SORCEROUS PLATES

A HIDDEN DISHES NOVELLA

TAO WONG

Sorcerous Plates

A Starlit Publishing Book
Published by Starlit Publishing

PO Box 30035
High Park PO
Toronto, ON
M6P 3K0
Canada

www.starlitpublishing.com

Ebook ISBN: 9781778552601

Print ISBN: 9781778552878

SORCEROUS PLATES

Contents

ONE

Rõõmu

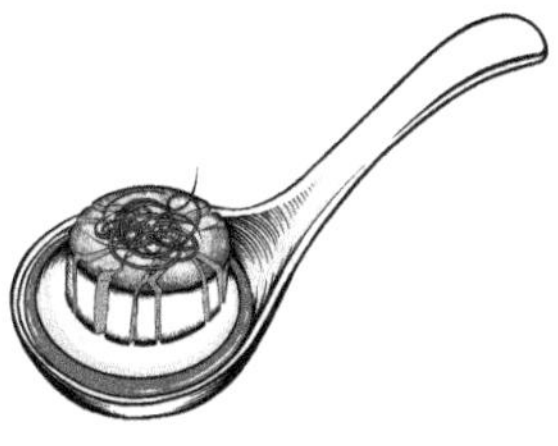

Mo Meng raised an eyebrow at Kelly, who was shifting side-to-side in her long, black cocktail dress. Little glittering sequins on the dress were accompanied by a clutch that could—maybe—hold her Presto card, a debit card and lipstick if she was being ambitious. He tried to keep his amusement off his face as the unseasonably cold early spring wind cut through the air, causing the pair to shiver.

She raised a foot and stamped down, wobbled a little as she tried to stand on too-high heels that pinched her feet and pitched her forward. He took hold of her hand for a moment, the smile wiped from his face as he recalled other women, once forced to totter around on uncomfortable or painful feet in the name of fashion.

"It's really not that bad," Kelly said quickly, in an attempt to mollify him and his sudden frown. "I don't understand why it's taking them so long to seat everyone, though. You'd think with so many waiters…"

"A matter of protocol, I think." Mo Meng shrugged. "Thank you, by the way, for coming."

"Are you kidding me?" she said, her voice rising enough that the others in line looked at her. She flushed a little, caught sight of a smirking glance an older man shot her and Mo Meng, and glared him down till he dropped whatever thoughts he was having about their age difference, before answering him. "It's *Bondu*. I've never eaten a multiple Michelin star chef's meal before. Of course I was coming when you invited me."

He smiled a little at Kelly's obvious excitement, then took a couple of necessary steps to cover the distance that had opened up when the next group ahead of them were seated.

"I've never been to the opening night of a new restaurant before, have you?" Kelly whispered, looking from side to side. The crowd was quite a mixture of social media influencers in glitzy, beautiful dresses and—more often than not—significant cleavage, the rich and important in business suits or luxurious comfort chic, and other chefs like Mo Meng. That last group was easy to pick out, since most were dressed up a little, but rarely bothered with full suits, certainly not tailored ones. Never mind the telltale marks of rough hands, the occasional burn on a forearm or a bandage around a finger. "Who am I kidding? Of course you have."

"A few," Mo Meng admitted. "Though this is not technically their opening, but a private event before the official launch."

"Right, that's *much* better," Kelly said, sarcastically. "I don't belong here..."

"You're my head of staff." At the unexpected title, Kelly's head snapped around from the casual perusal of others to fix on the old wizard, who seemed entirely ignorant of the consternation his words had caused. "If I'm here, you have every right to be."

"Just as long as no one thinks I'm your arm candy..." If she were, she would not be unusual, since that was another distinct group, most often hanging off the arms of the rich and important. Not a clientele that visited the Nameless Restaurant, not for the most part. Trudging through an alleyway was just not exclusive enough for most of that sort, never mind the fact that they had to wait in line, or the lack of good lighting for pictures. Add in how crowded the tables were, and it didn't even make much sense for a romantic dating experience—unless one's shared love was food.

There was something in the way Mo Meng nodded at her words that had Kelly narrowing her eyes at him. "What? You aren't a cradle robber, are you?"

"I'd point out that most of you are, by a significant degree, my juniors. There's only a few who might be considered peers, and even then..." He shrugged. "A few hundred years one way or the other often separate us."

"But there are degrees. Maturity!"

"Obviously, maturity matters," Mo Meng said. "But once upon a time, fourteen-year-olds ruled kingdoms and led tribes to war. Some of them were better rulers than their older counterparts." A small smile. "Though, funnily enough, people forget that peasants and farmers generally married later. What is true for the upper class was not always the same for those below."

"Forced maturity is not good for a child."

"Be careful about labeling individuals children. Some might take offense, or point out that from a certain point of view, all of you are too." His lips twitched up in a wry smile. "So long as both parties are of sound mind, aren't coerced and are making a decision with full understanding of what is to come, what we consider an appropriate age range for relationships isn't really our business."

"I should have known you were a dirty old man." She smiled to take the sting out of her words.

"Robbing an individual of agency by enforcing our preconceived notions of their place is just as bad. Marriage—or relationships—with the rich and powerful has been a long-standing method of raising one's status." He shrugged. "It might not be fair, but we don't complain when a man joins the army to succeed either, and if anything, the sale of their body to the government can have even worse long-standing effects."

"I guess... I just..." Kelly shook her head. "It's creepy."

Mo Meng acknowledged her feelings with a nod, content to let the discussion die. He had done his part, challenging her thinking. Not that he did not agree with her in part. There were limits, degrees of separation that should be enforced—if not by an individual, then society—so that the vulnerable might not be preyed upon. That kind of peer pressure could be wielded to keep others in check. Of course, such things could—and did—fail far too often.

Silence lingered for a little while longer, as the pair shuffled closer. Talking about such topics—or giving hints about his age—did not bother Mo Meng much. The hidden world was hidden, not because a steel wall was drawn across their interactions, but because the soft curtains of obliviousness and self-interest kept others from listening in. Add in a healthy dash of skepticism and the surplus of movies, TV shows and even make-believe games, and most were as happy to discard the odd tidbit of overheard secrets as to pursue it.

As for those who did pursue it and held no malice in their hearts? They were accepted into the fold of the hidden world, with little concern or objection. There was always enough space for everyone, if one chose to offer it.

"How did you get on this list, anyway?" Kelly asked, as they neared the hostess.

Mo Meng fished in the pocket of his tunic, finding the invitation in the inner pocket of the modified robes he wore. He had ordered this work from

China, grateful to note that the new trend in modern hanfu made his own preference for such clothing no longer as notable.

Also, rather more practical, with less annoyingly long and elaborate sleeves.

"I once knew the chef. A long time ago, when he first started out. Before I had my own restaurant, even."

"Then, how...?"

Before he could explain, the hostess was there, checking over the invitation, gesturing for the pair to follow the waiter. She led them into the building with a smile, turning away to greet the next guests as the pair were let in, the glowing light of the restaurant Rõõmu shining down on them in cool blue and white.

Two
Seating Arrangements

The interior of the Rõõmu was as different from the Nameless Restaurant as one could get, and still serve the same function. The Rõõmu was a modern design in a building purpose-chosen near the Toronto waterfront so that it could catch all the light of a long summer evening, so that the sparkle of the water in the distance and the noise of the passing traffic was muted by large, floor-length, triple-paned windows.

Lights—bright, but not too -bright—lingered high above, shedding a soft yellow illumination over everything. White -walls—cream really, not sterile, hospital white—and modern industrial chic with exposed vents and fire suppression devices gave the restaurant a modern, warehouse vibe, while the white tableware and exquisitely pressed and waxed tablecloths sat, present in military precision before each seat.

The chairs were tall, light steel furnishings, a carefully chosen padded leather seat ensuring comfort. A small sway in the back of the seat allowed one to rest even more comfortably in the chair. No rickety chairs taken from a dumpster or hundred-year-old antiques salvaged from some forgotten restaurant here.

Even the waiters were pressed and pressured, ramrod straight in strict, white uniforms and black pants. Kelly drank in the sights, blue eyes wide, lips a little parted as she drifted along beside Mo Meng. There was so much to see and experience, from the light floral scents that pervaded the building thanks to the fresh cut flowers and the planters artfully arranged to block views and break up noise, to the thrum of voices and the light, almost inaudible hum of the straining air conditioning.

A blink, a slow one, as realization struck her. She turned to look at Mo Meng, his return look glimmering with understanding humor. His magic had been so subtle she had not recognized the relief from the heat he had cast over her outside, released once they swept into the building.

For a man who said that he disliked utilizing magic, the variety and types that she came across regularly was staggering. Always tiny charms, minor cantrips that eased life just a touch, and were often missed by others.

"It seems we are not the only ones taking the night off," Mo Meng murmured under his breath as the waiter pulled out Kelly's chair for her. She took the seat, turning to spot a familiar figure dressed in full tails. A swarthy complexion, a long, slender figure, a charming smile, and a woman that had graced the cover of *Vogue* magazinea bare few months ago for Paris fashion week.

A flicker of irritation that she quickly squashed, even as she continued to struggle to understand why it bothered her. Why he even worked in their restaurant, when he could so easily afford so many other things.

"This is why you closed the restaurant?" The voice was low and sultry. Coming from another, it might have further annoyed Kelly, but she found it hard to be upset with the raven-haired, tanned goddess standing by their table, her attention focused on her dinner companion. "I'm hurt."

"You're here," Mo Meng pointed out.

"Only because you closed up!" Marilyn di Rossi sniffed, the tight purple dress that showcased all her ample curves hugging her body with each movement. "What did you expect me to do when you're gone?"

"Eat somewhere else, of course."

"Exactly!" A small gesture to the waiters who bustled over, rearranging the table as they added another place setting to theirs without asking. "They almost told me they had no space. No space. For me!"

"I'm sure you *charmed* your way into what you wanted," Kelly's boss drawled.

"Well, of course." Taking the seat proffered by the waiter, she lounged, placing a hand on Mo Meng's shoulder. "But you need not worry, I only wielded my other forms of influence."

"What other forms?" Kelly assumed that Marilyn meant she had not used her glamour ability as a vampire.

"Money, my dear. And connections." An idle wave. "I sent one of those uppity brats away to eat at Blue, under my name of course. I also promised to pay for a dinner here, later."

"That was...generous."

"A trifling thing."

Kelly twitched, but kept silent. She was growing used to the olds, how easily they spoke of such things, as though a few hundred dollars was nothing to them. It probably wasn't, not when their worth was likely in the tens or hundreds of millions.

"Can we expect any of the others?" she asked instead.

"I doubt it. Tobias mentioned something about organizing a clan dinner instead, and Jotun dislikes such events. He thinks it is all flash, and certainly they never provide enough food for him."

Before they could speak, a waiter came by, offering a wine menu for their choosing. At the same time, he checked in on their preference for water—sparkling, flat, tap, and some specific brands. It made Kelly's head spin a little, but Marilyn answered for the group with ease, sending the waiter off to acquire some sparkling water with a very European name.

"Ice Giant metabolisms run low, compared to most giants, but it's still significant," Mo Meng said, softly. "At least he's not the cloud kind. They have to work with teams of personal chefs just to keep themselves fed in the human world."

"Really?" It was rare for them to talk about such things. Mostly, Kelly had found her knowledge of the hidden world coming slowly and in pieces.

"Ever watch eating competitions?" Marilyn asked.

"I have. You don't mean...?"

"Once. They used to dominate them, before it was ruled unfair to everyone else," Marilyn said. "Nowadays, we have our own kinds where they can compete with others of their sort." She shook her head. "It's like that, a lot of the time. We have our own competitions, our own events."

"Like a supernatural Olympics?"

The vampire nodded. "You can imagine the trouble we had, organizing that one. Nocturnal and diurnal races, working the limits and ranges, figuring out the rules."

"We?" Kelly said, admiringly.

"I had some small part in it. Mostly in dance."

"There's no dance in the Olympics." Kelly paused, then added. "Well, not unless you count breaking..."

"More's the pity," she sniffed. "We made sure there was in ours. There's no reason why there can't be some elegance to such a sweaty and aggressive event, after all. You'd be surprised at the level of cross-pollination. And of course I helped organize the first balls."

"Why don't you now?"

"Too much work," Marilyn replied. "It's good to give back, but it's better to make sure the young have a chance to grow too. If those of us who have done it all before continue to keep those positions, there's never any change. The youth have nowhere to go, no chances to fail. Anyway..."

"Some of us like to rest too," Mo Meng muttered. "Always being in charge, after a while you learn when to say enough is enough."

"Or you should, at least."

"True. But if we let them make their mistakes, you never know what they might come up with."

"Like this restaurant," Kelly said, looking around. "It's very different from ours."

"Very different markets and goals," Mo Meng said. "Until recently, mine was never meant for more than a few friends..."

Before Kelly could stop and ask him if he regretted it, the waiter swept over to interrupt the group once again, to fill their glasses and take their wine order. At the same time, as she listened with half an ear to what Mo Meng asked, she noted that the rest of the clientele had finally been seated.

It seemed dinner would begin, soon enough.

THREE

Whetting the Appetite

The first dish to arrive was not truly a dish, but the bread that such restaurants always seemed determined to provide. Fresh-baked, more often than not in-house, and provided sliced with an accompaniment; one could often tell a lot from what kind of bread and what form it came in.

Large quantities of breadsticks, or with seasoning or condiments on the bread itself, such as cheese, to differentiate oneself. Bread rolls that might have been purchased in bulk and were easy to serve to others, or baked in-house and presented either one per diner or in groups. Big, rustic loaves sliced thick for dipping, with accompaniments.

The accompaniments, those were another indicator. Olive oil and vinegar, when one wanted to signal a Mediterranean experience: Italian or Greek or the like, and the quality of the oil and vinegar itself put to the test. Or perhaps butter. Coming in plastic serving packages, bought by the bagful, thrown in a freezer and still hard, or taken out and left to reach room temperature, so that the butter pats—or margarine perhaps—were spreadable.

In higher-end restaurants, in places that cared, the butter might come in curls, stripped from the sticks of butter so as to soften and spread more easily. In a place like this, though, the butter might not even be bought from local farmers but made in-house, though few would churn it themselves; but breakdown work taken from a trusted source.

Mo Meng understood the large amount of work involved. Fresh milk, brought to factories, pasteurized and then either processed and packaged or processed into cream, cheese or butter. At a glance, it was easy to tell that these butter patties, formed into tiny squares across the plate, were made in-house. A richer color, a more vibrant sheen to them.

He wondered what they did with the buttermilk, the other product of working with heavy cream. He assumed, somewhere on the menu, there was deep fried chicken. It would make sense, since the –meat—pre-soaked overnight in buttermilk—would be moister, juicier and tastier if done that way.

A small trick he had once showed his former student.

Having made sure the bread and butter were properly placed on the table, the waiter now spoke with authority and a smile on his lips. "The bread is a seven-grain sourdough, made in-house by our award-winning baker. The starter dates from the eighteenth century, passed on by the chef's own family from the East Coast. We bake the bread every morning in-house, just like the butter is made in our own kitchens. The chef is talking about selling small patties in the future, though we are currently building up our supply."

"It's not just salt in there, is it?" Kelly said.

"Not at all, miss. We have three varieties of butter at the moment. The first is a garlic butter, with parsley, roasted garlic and garlic salt added. While it might sound strong, we believe you'll find that it only enhances the flavor of the bread.

"The second item there, slightly darker than the others, is our cinnamon butter, which is sweeter than the other two for those wanting a contrast with our bread. And finally, we have a red wine and shallot butter."

"You said 'at the moment'?" Marilyn asked, sweetly.

"Yes, miss." The waiter inclined their head. "The chef intends to rotate some of the butters as the season demands it. You'll find that while some items will be permanently on the menu, many will be rotated to suit local growing patterns and the weather."

"You aren't going to commit to the five-mile idea, are you?" Marilyn asked, no challenge in her voice but certainly in her eyes.

"That is a chef's decision, miss; but I believe we intend to keep it as local as possible, without limiting ourselves entirely." The waiter gestured down to the food, smiling. "Please, enjoy."

Mo Meng chuckled a little as the man escaped the sharp tongue of Marilyn, who turned a look on him.

"Come now, let them be. It's not like many of them understand how much has changed," Mo Meng said.

"What do you mean?" Kelly asked.

He pointed to the butter, waved a hand around idly to encompass Old Town and maybe even St. Lawrence market, that permanent farmer's market and food stall not so far from them. "Many of the herbs we take for granted, the plants and dishes we eat, did not originally originate from the places we think they do." At the puzzled look, he tapped the bread. "Wheat was grown in Europe, not North America. Potatoes came from the 'new world' but became synonymous with European cuisine. Rice, obviously, came more from Asia, but did you know that the breed of pig we eat comes from China? Tomatoes were North America, chilis from central and south America; not India, if you can imagine that."

"You would not believe how dull cuisine was, before the sixteenth century." Marilyn's nose wrinkled a little. "How much fat and jellies, and the variety of birds that we ate—swans and geese and peacocks even—because it was a way to show strength."

"I..." Kelly hesitated, ducked her head. "So that's why you don't like the 'eat local' movement?"

A shrug from the vampire. "There is nothing wrong with it, so long as they do not grow too enamored with their own marketing."

"If anything, limitations can improve one's creativity," Mo Meng said. "But perhaps we should talk less and eat more?"

Plucking a slice of bread from the bowl, he set it down on the small plate provided. Rather than reach for the butters, he tore off a piece of the bread to taste it, inspecting the bread itself first. Thick and dark white, the mixed-grain sourdough was fluffy with near consistent holes and a hard crust. He ran a fingernail down the side of the crust, noted the stiffness and the slight cracking before popping the piece into his mouth.

Saliva—already flowing from the smell of fresh bread, likely reheated just briefly before being served—met the bread, his tongue curling up a little at the hint of sourness left from the yeast. He was not a personal fan of such bread himself, preferring a blander or more sugary version; but he understood the preference for them.

This bread was soft on the inside, with crunch in the crust but not too hard. Not overbaked, so that it was impossible to bite through without significant liquid and a strong jaw, but fresh, with the texture of partly cooked and whole grains filling his mouth.

Once, and then again, he masticated the piece before swallowing, turning now to the butters. From the richer color, he could tell they had used a heavier cream, a European version—82% fat—rather than the heavy cream that was made in North America. Very good for spreading over bread and for a richer taste.

Terrible for one's figure.

Mo Meng started with the garlic and herb butter, often used on top of steaks to give the meat a deeper flavor and make lean meats richer. Modern cuisine decried the use of fat, forgetting that half their problems came from the additional sugars added to their food from a variety of sources. Corn syrup, sugar tossed into everything from coffee to pasta sauce to milk.

All the while, the body hungered for fat, remembering tens of thousands of years of desperate need for calories. When humankind's greatest danger was starvation and times of famine, when it happened so often that certain sub-groups preselected for individuals who could survive constant famines.

Garlic butter, a burst of flavor mixing with the sourness, went down smoothly, just a hint of fresh parsley lingering in his mouth, the taste washed away moments later by water. Lingering for a moment, before he chewed on a fresh piece of bare bread.

From garlic to the next in line, his eyes half-closing as he savored the cinnamon. Sweet, of course, he had been deploring that—but he understood the attraction. Cinnamon, smoky and heavy in his mouth, sugar and fats mixing with the bread, drowning out the sour. He chewed, savoring the flavor, thought it was perhaps too much of a contrast for his tastes.

Savory might be a better choice; but there was one more...

Or perhaps not.

He stared at the empty patty spot, missing the last item. Turned to stare at a pair of guilty faces, and realized perhaps there was a winner amongst the three.

Four
Bread & Garlic Butter

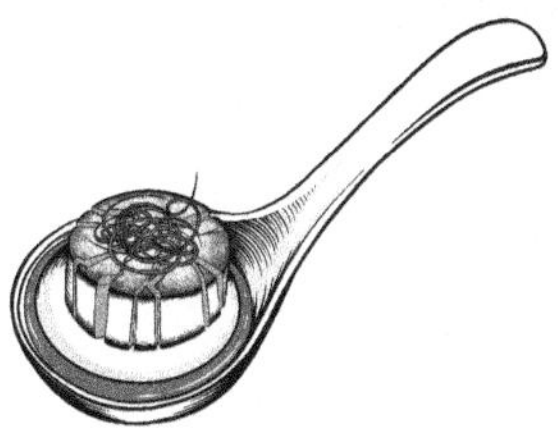

Listening to Mo Meng and Marilyn discuss their past and the world gone by had been interesting, but it meant that she was forced to wait while the bread sat there, so tantalizingly. Kelly had meant to have a snack before coming here, just enough to keep her stomach from complaining; but then she had started studying, her mom had called, and then the group chat in Econ 301 had exploded about who was sleeping with who and...

Well, she had dressed, gotten her makeup on and scrambled through Toronto traffic to get here on time. An extra delay on Line 1, due to some issue on Union, had caused further delays and she had no time to eat anything. Now she was salivating at the smell of bread and wondering if it was rude to just start.

The moment the pair finally fell silent and started taking pieces of bread, she had fallen on it with all the grace of a stunned bird. Unlike Mo Meng who seemed intent on tasting everything individually, she had slathered butter on heavily, testing from the opposite side first.

It was surprising to her how even a small change, the addition of herbs or garlic or flavored salt to something as everyday as butter, could make such a difference. The bread, soft and spongy, with a good mouthfeel and springiness, was flooded with the extra strong butter taste, filling her mouth with the fats, the salts and herbs.

Garlic butter to begin, then after that piece was gone, the cinnamon butter that reminded her of hot chocolate drinks at Christmas and cinnamon bran muffins. Tasty, but not what she was looking for, so she moved on quickly to the last portion, the red wine and shallot.

Lightly roasted shallots—a smaller root vegetable, similar to an onion but sweeter and sharper in taste—were braised in red wine and then blended into the butter, so that the taste was uniform through the spread. When added to the bread, it brought a fuller, mildly sweet aspect to the sourdough. One that had her lips turning up with each bite.

Moments later, she was scooping up another portion, adding it to her bread with a deft flick of her hand. As she looked up while popping the freshly buttered bread into her mouth, she caught the glinting amusement in Marilyn's eyes as the woman copied her actions, taking a large dollop onto her slice.

Eyes narrowing, Kelly reached and cut off as generous an amount herself, taking another portion of bread onto her plate. All the while, she chewed, mouth flooded with the rich wine, hints of bramble and a touch of spice along with the sweetness of the shallots, a counterpoint to the sourness of the bread. On occasion, she'd bite into the crust, the crack of hardened bread echoing in her mouth.

Spread, spread, bite, chew. Swallow.

Spread, spread, bite, chew, chew, swallow.

Spread...

No more butter, and an annoyed boss staring at the absence of the red wine. She swallowed around a suddenly dry mouth, as she considered pointing and shouting 'she did it', before offering instead as an excuse:

"It was good!"

"Obviously," Mo Meng said, dryly. "I'll have to try the same myself. Though it'd be easier to recreate it, if I had tasted it first..."

"You could ask for more?"

"I could." Picking up the glass of bubble water, he sipped it again and grimaced, then waved down the waiter. Moments later, he had an order for simple, flat water.

"You don't like the water?" Marilyn said.

"I've never been a fan of carbonated water." His nose wrinkled. "Or the kind from the springs. You can always taste the earth it's passed through, and it can mar the taste of your meal. Glacier water at least is somewhat more neutral, I find. And the lack of bubbles means it doesn't alter the properties of the food."

"Well, I like it. It gives a nice pop to the dish. You should add some to your restaurant."

Mo Meng shook his head and Kelly hid a little smile. It was funny, how he would add seasonal or topical drinks like kefir or lassi or even certain types of flavored water—limes and lemons in his filtered water system—but he disliked bubbly. However, as much as he might protest, Kelly had noted how such thoughts would sink into his mind when voiced by a customer, eventually making their way out.

Sometimes in a different form—the kefir was one such example, in her view. Though she was certain he would add to it at some point, perhaps via magic if he disliked the technology; or perhaps by visiting some of his friends.

That number seemed both extensive and sparse. Her boss had a network of contacts, people who knew of him, who owed him or came to him for enchantments and spells; but at the same time, he seemed to live a lonely life. An existence focused around his kitchen, his dishes, and the neighborhoods around the city.

No international jaunts, no world-wide tours. No visits to far-flung vacation spots or lazy hours on a tropical beach. Her eyes slid left, to Marilyn—thinking that she was similar. For all her glitz and glamor—and yes, she did still go to New York and Paris and London—she was at the restaurant more often than not.

At least Damian was living his supernatural life, even if it was a playboy one.

"You're staring again, dear," Marilyn murmured gently to her.

Kelly startled, not before Damian caught her eye and smiled. She flushed, tore her gaze away and looked at Marilyn, two burning spots on her cheeks. "I... It's not what you're thinking! I was just thinking..."

"Of course you were." Eyes twinkling, Marilyn added, "Thinking and looking is good, but you might wish to turn your looks and mind elsewhere. He is, by definition one might say, a bad boy."

"He's not that bad!" Kelly said, defensively. "He's more of a...a..."

"Playboy socialite," Mo Meng muttered. "Billionaire, playboy socialite. Except he isn't a tech genius or much of a philanthropist." Rubbing his chin, Mo Meng added. "At least he's not an arms dealer."

"You..." Kelly eyes narrowed. "You researched those?"

"Eventually," he replied.

"Anyway, he's not that bad. He's quite disciplined and organized at work, now that he's worked it out."

"We're not saying he's bad," Marilyn said, softly. "Just that he's... hmm... potentially bad news."

"Some might say your kind are too."

"Bad press," Marilyn sniffed. "And, well, some younger members not having much control." A head turned away, as she looked at passing waiters, staring at the surrounding groups. "And a bad time, when technology couldn't help us. Many of us regret what we had to do..."

Kelly blinked, then put a hand on Marilyn's hand, squeezing it quickly. "He hasn't done anything to regret yet, has he?"

"Not that we know of," Mo Meng said.

"Then maybe we should give him the benefit of the doubt."

"That's a big benefit..." Marilyn replied. "The potential..."

"How many times has that line been used? How many priests, how many governments?" He sighed. "It's easy to talk about what-ifs, but if we feared all who might do evil, we would have to begin with children and end with ourselves. For us, who have already done worse..."

"Worse?" Kelly said.

Mo Meng smiled, tiredly. "We all have pasts, my dear. And regrets."

Before she could follow up, the waiter appeared, first to refill their glasses, and then to take away the empty bread and butter dishes. He paused as he did so, using a white cloth to sweep up the fallen breadcrumbs that marred the tablecloth, ensuring it was clean and clear before departing. Another waiter arrived moments later to take their plates.

The signal, it seemed, for the next course.

FIVE

Amuse-Bouche

T he waiter glided over, a trio of plates held expertly in his hands. Small plates, no bigger than the bread plates that had been taken not long ago, each with a single angled, white soup spoon on it. Inside the spoon was the amuse-bouche that was being served, from what Kelly could tell.

A small scallop—about the size of a quarter—expertly cooked, lay on top of a clear, white base; a jelly of some sort. To add color, spring onion tops and arugula were artfully placed on the scallop, a drizzle of red sauce drawing lines on the dish and the plate beneath.

"Pretty," Kelly murmured as it was set down beside her.

"It is," Marilyn agreed. "They certainly do take care to improve the look of their dishes." She shot a quick glance at the quiet Mo Meng who was having his plate placed before him, artfully turned so that the spoon was in the correct position for him to pick up. "You could do more of this."

"I could," Mo Meng said, carefully. "Plating is important. And we do the basics." He tapped the plate. "We wipe the food down, make sure the plates are warm, put the garnishes on top. I even take a few moments to twirl the pasta or ensure it's properly set-up."

"But no mounds, nothing artful."

"Who has the time?" Mo Meng said, sniffily. "You do know I'm the only one working the kitchen, right?"

"You could hire help." Marilyn let the word linger before she added, "Again."

"Again?" Kelly mouthed the word, then blinked, remembering whose restaurant they were in. Mo Meng had mentioned that the chef had previously worked for him for a little while. "Oh... That sounds good."

"I had help with the basics, not with the cooking." He sniffed. "I don't want too much more help. We're already too busy as it is."

Kelly had to quietly agree with her boss. Sure, it was nice to get more tips. Even if the boss paid a decent, livable wage and then some, and there were signs in the restaurant to indicate no tipping, no one actually paid attention to that. The supernaturals seemed to think it was a matter of course, a necessity to keep on the establishment's good side, and the mortals—for the most part—were so used to tipping everywhere else, they did it here too.

"So keep the wait list, but more help would mean less work for you."

"Training is work."

Listening to the pair argue over what seemed to be well-trodden ground, Kelly turned instead to the amuse-bouche. She picked up the spoon, raising it to eye level first and eyeing the entire thing. It was meant to be an appetite refresher, to hint at not just the food that was to come, but the way the chef would take the dining journey.

Or so she'd read. Hard to tell, sometimes, how much on the internet was real; especially when AI programs kept infiltrating results, offering their algorithmic word-selection choice answer to questions, rather than actual logic or knowledge.

No, she had no desire to put glue on pizza to keep the cheese from falling off, thank you.

"Seafood, for sure. And cream?" Kelly muttered. "Fresh greens."

"Consommé." Mo Meng interrupted his argument. "What you think of as cream is a consommé—a clear soup made from broth, boiled down further and clarified. It should give us a clear indicator of the flavor profile we can expect."

"Umami heavy, probably." Nose wrinkled a little, Marilyn copied Kelly's actions. "Smells light and airy, though."

Kelly nodded, considering what had been said. A seafood-heavy evening, then, with a dash of greens and perhaps lighter-palate fare. She could deal with that. In fact, she might even prefer it to a heavier meal. Though she wouldn't mind tasting some of the more expensive ingredients out there, like caviar.

She did draw the line at foie gras, though.

Placing the spoon in her mouth, she bit down, slicing through the fresh, tender scallop with her bare teeth. She found the action easy, only slight resistance offered by the scallop as she sliced through the tender meat before breaking the surface tension of the consommé, the jelly-like substance parting with even less resistance. A minor tilt of head and spoon let both freed portions slide through her mouth, where the consommé, mixing with the saliva in her mouth and rising in temperature, broke apart immediately, flooding her mouth.

Sweet was her first thought, but not in the overpowering way of processed sugar, but with the natural sugars of various vegetables—carrots, onions, perhaps something more. The taste was, as Marilyn had surmised, light—subtle in the amount of sugar, salt, broth. Chicken and seafood would be her guess, with perhaps mushroom in there too.

The red sauce was a very light chili sauce, maybe combined with red beets. Sweet and hot, but the heat was more a hint—the seeds stripped from the chili before it was added, so that only the memory of the burn that could have been there remained.

Rather than overpowering, it was refreshing and made her mouth water, even as she began chewing on the scallop meat. Fresh scallops were always a treat, cooked well with a hint of the sea still in them. Within moments, the bite was gone and she had to finish the second, finding that the second bite layered further in her mouth.

A wonderful rush of sensations, bright, fresh sea, with hints of a heavier meal, the touch of greenery and the chicken bringing a more grounded layer to the meal. With a sigh of disappointment, Kelly set the spoon on her tiny plate.

Excited now, Kelly looked around, curious about what else the restaurant had to offer. An appetite refresher indeed.

She certainly wanted more.

SIX

An Unexpected Visitor

T he plates and utensils were taken away, replaced with pristine, shiny new sets. The table swept clean with quick, efficient movements that removed not an iota of dirt, as the table was clean as it stood, and yet the waiter took the time to double-check and wipe it down. More water was added to glasses, topping them off with efficient movements before their table was left alone again.

Mo Meng tilted his head to the side, eyes dancing across the group of socialites, businessmen and influencers that took up the place. He soaked in the atmosphere, noted the way that the noise level in the restaurant was a touch higher than he would have preferred for a busy restaurant evening. While there was a low-level song playing, some jazz number that he could not name or place, to help break up the noise and conversation, it was the lack of wood and the plethora of hard surfaces and exposed concrete ceilings that helped bounce the noise around.

Funny, how a place like his own with its exposed brickwork could be quieter, but it had a lot, he now knew, to do with his own preference for wood and the shelving along walls, utilized to have familiar and useful jars and other ingredients within reach for later use; but also, to break up the sound waves.

He did note the addition of greenery, the various plants that helped shade and hide, also muting the noise level compared to some of the other more modern, sleek factory-chic restaurant designs that were now the rage. Metal and plastic and exposed metal piping with minimal soft cloth led to some truly painful and uncomfortable experiences; though less so in proper Michelin starred restaurants. At least the Western-style ones, that focused on a soft, luxurious ambience and white tablecloths.

"Your thoughts?" Marilyn said.

"A little noisy." Mo Meng frowned. "I should add some greenery to the restaurant."

"We have asked you to before. I recall a particular dryad mentioning that it would be a nice change compared to your overuse of her cousins," the vampire teased. "I'm sure she—or a cousin of hers—would be happy to come back and help with the addition."

"I could pay them in meals..." Mo Meng mused.

"Are dryads carnivores, then?" Kelly asked, curiously.

"Mmm, some are. Some are omnivores, others are strict vegetarians," Marilyn said. "Like everything else, there's variations and individuality."

"And the majority?"

"Carnivores." The pair replied at the same time, looked at one another and then at Kelly before breaking out in laughter at the look on her face.

"I..." Kelly frowned. "It wasn't what I expected."

"When they take on a physical body, they seem to delight in testing what they haven't been able to experience. It's why they're so...physical," Mo Meng replied. "Plant spirits end up more sensual, enjoying the activity of a moving, fleshly body in all its ways. Including consuming meat."

"But not plants?"

"They prefer meat. Plants do eat plants sometimes, or the rough equivalent. Parasitic plants are not uncommon, after all."

"Oh..."

"I was more curious about your thoughts on the amuse-bouche," Marilyn said.

"Are you looking forward to the next dish?" he asked instead of replying.

"Yes."

"More than when you first started."

"Yes..."

"Then it did its job, did it not?" Mo Meng said. "Whatever other thoughts I might have are unimportant."

"Surely you have something to say," Marilyn muttered.

"Bondu's always been a little leery of vegetables," Mo Meng said. "I'm glad to see that has changed a bit, though some might consider spring onion not a change at all."

"We're going to be eating seafood too, are we not?" Kelly said, looking around the place. "The consommé was quite light, so... does he intend it to be mostly seafood? That's considered light."

"Seafood, pasta, maybe some chicken or pork," Marilyn replied. "That would be my guess."

"How many dishes do you think there will be, then?" Kelly said, counting off her fingers as she looked around. "Are we getting half a dozen small plates? Or the usual?"

Mo Meng shrugged. He waved a hand towards the waiter who was hovering not far away, watching the tables. "If you really want to know, you can ask him."

"Or we can wait, enjoying the anticipation," Marilyn said, stilling Kelly with a single raised hand. "That is, if you can do patience."

"I can." She crossed her fingers in front of her, then after a moment unlaced them sheepishly to take a sip of water.

"Good. Patience and learning to live in the moment is important in the supernatural world. You might notice, most of us move slower than the modern world."

"Except when eating," Kelly said with a smirk. "I've seen how you all finish your food."

"Blame that on him." She pointed. "It's just too good."

Kelly laughed softly, while Mo Meng smiled. "There's no need to teach her too much about us. She should learn how to live in the real world, not ours."

"Why not?" Kelly said.

"It's better, overall. The more you get drawn in, the more complicated things can get." He ran one finger along the table, sighed and looked toward the doors. "Case in point..."

Moments later, a man pushed in, smiling and waving at the hostess who kept trying to get in his way. He was not a particularly tall man, Chinese in origin and unlike most of those here, clad in a simple t-shirt and jeans combination. Kelly noted that he was rather well muscled, though, carrying himself with easy confidence as he kept speaking. "Really, I'll just be a moment. I just need to talk to someone—!"

"Sir, this is a private event. Private. You can't come in!"

"I just need one...! There. See, he's right there." The man leaned one way, as though to edge around the hostess who shuffled over, only to realize she had been faked out moments later as he darted around her and strode past. To Kelly's surprise, she realized he was headed straight for them, only for a waiter to step in his way. "Oh, come on! One second. Think of me as a really persistent messenger. I drop off the message, I leave you all in peace."

"Sir, if you do not leave, we will make you do so." The waiter, not even the tallest of them, put a hand on the intruder's chest, as though to push him away.

"Master..." The boy turned, raised an eyebrow and ignored the hand on his chest entirely. A lip curled, but before the man could lose his temper, Mo Meng spoke up.

"Let him in," Mo Meng said. "He's my guest."

"You already have one, sir..."

"Ask your owner. Tell him that we need to add one more." There was a note in Mo Meng's voice that Kelly had never heard before, something aloof and commanding. It cut through the man's protests, daring him to contradict Mo Meng.

Moments later, one of the older waiters pulled the impertinent one back and muttered softly, leaving not long after for the kitchen. In the meantime, released from the altercation, the intruder finally wandered over to their table.

"Master Mo," the intruder bowed, "thank you for your help. I have a small matter I must speak with you about. Semi-urgently." Then, looking around, he added. "Privately."

Only when he bowed a little, as he stood there in the light, did she recall the man. She turned toward the entrance, curious to see if the other would arrive, and was only a little disappointed when the doorway stayed empty.

SEVEN

Strange Patrons

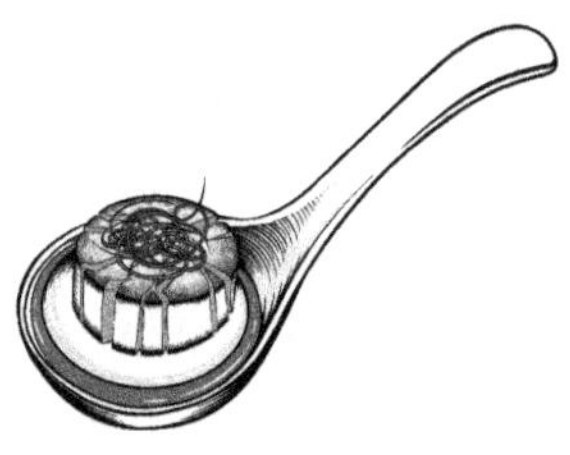

A vampire, a master magician and a waitress sat at a table. It was the start of the strangest joke Henry could think of, except it was not even the strangest group he had dealt with in the last few years. Not since a jinn had wandered into his life after he purchased and cleaned the wrong ring. Certainly not since he had freed her, once and for all, like a Disney hero, and caused all the havoc that was emerging in the world now.

Was it a surprise, then, that he felt drawn to solving some of those problems? To smoothing out the rough interactions of supernatural and mortal denizens of the world? He did not think so, no matter what Lily might say.

"Come, sit, join us." Mo Meng gestured to the empty chair, an inviting smile on his lips. Henry noted that it only reached the lips, though, the quiet reserve in his eyes leaking none of his true feelings.

"I cannot, I have matters to attend to. I just need to ask a few things..." Henry began, only to see a hand raised.

"Sit. Even questing heroes must rest at some point. And I certainly don't intend to give up my evening off, so you might as well enjoy dinner and ask your questions."

"I—" Before he could object further, a –waiter—the same one that had –disappeared—arrived. He was all smiles now, waving the others away and pulling the chair out.

"Sir, if you will sit, we will ensure that the amuse-bouche is delivered post-haste so as not to disrupt the flow of dinner for the rest of the guests." The tone was polite; the words, however, were pointed.

"Please, sit." The waitress, bright-eyed, smiling and with streaks of pink in her hair, asked him again. He found himself sitting down, never able to say no to a pretty woman. A troublesome problem, when so many of the supernatural were—naturally or unnaturally—gorgeous.

"Henry Tsin, is it not?" Marilyn, the vampire with raven-dark hair, dark red dress and plunging neckline murmured. He kept his gaze locked upwards, inclining his head in acknowledgement. "Marilyn di Rossi. You are the companion of that one, Lily, is it not?"

"Sometime companion," Henry said, pushing aside his impatience. He had to remember, they were of the old kind. These games of question and answer, of polite small talk, were important to them. He would get nowhere by insisting on his way, not just yet. "She goes where she wishes, and I try to follow when I can."

"A maid, then. A handyman fixing problems," Mo Meng said, though contrary to his words, his tone was not unkind.

"She's not that bad. She doesn't destroy anything or cause havoc on purpose."

"It's just what she is," Mo Meng confirmed. "That's what most of their kind are. It's part and parcel of their nature, no different than a shifter's change during the full moon or a knocker's desire to help. Just something to be managed, yes."

"So where is she?" Kelly asked, curiously. "Is she coming?"

"No, she's in Panama right now." At the frown sent his way, he could not help but shrug. "She's lazing on a beach, saying she wants—needs—to get a tan. And that the Middle East has gotten too sandy for her liking."

"But she's on a beach," Kelly said, puzzled.

"Exactly."

For a moment she stared in incomprehension before breaking out into quite fetching giggles. He found himself smiling too, grateful that there was at least someone who understood. Dealing with the powers and their foolishness was taxing to the extreme.

He understood it, to some extent. They walked with shadows of the past at all times, memories of bygone ages and people. More so for people like Lily, who had lived longer than any of them, had seen entire countries rise and fall and the very environment that she had grown up in alter beyond belief. So that she could no longer recognize the very lands she had once walked.

Never mind that many of her memories were fractured, her experience of the outside world splotchy as her former owners might utilize

–her—or not—as necessary. There were entire periods in which she had been cast aside, hidden away because of the danger that her very presence might engender.

Much of the sixteenth century onwards was like that, when the decline of magic had truly begun. Only in the late eighteenth had she been taken out, the return of magic coming fitfully and in jumps, as fascination with the occult grew and her own legend faded.

"Your amuse-bouche," a voice intoned stiffly. The plate was deposited before him, a small thing of scallop and jelly, and he frowned. Not that he had anything against seafood, but he was beginning to realize how hungry he truly was.

A mouthful later, he was—briefly—sated, grateful for the start of a meal, though he wished they had brought the bread back out. His stomach, newly awakened, roiled a little, reminding him that his last meal had been in the early morning hours, a croissant taken from a bakeshop before driving to Toronto, crossing a border and having to charm—literally and magically—his way past customs officials.

Annoying that they were beginning to grow ever stricter, with new additions to the border to detect the flow of supernaturals and block them. Chatter on the grapevine was that half the –turnarounds—the ones that never made the news—kept from crossing into the US were working supernaturals, caught and refused entry because of their nature.

"You look troubled," Kelly said softly. "The food not to your liking?"

"Mmmm?" Henry frowned, then looked at the table, licked his lips as he considered the sauce and the taste. "No, it was fine."

"Fine..." Mo Meng drawled. "I think if my own dishes were called that, I would be quite upset."

"I'm sorry, I didn't really come here to eat. I just have a question for you." He nodded to Mo Meng.

"So you said." Henry noted the glare that Kelly sent the magician chef's way, the look he gave her and then, like an indulgent uncle, the smile. "Fine. What is it that you want to know?"

"It's about uhh..." He looked around, dropped his voice a little. "Magic. A spell formula actually. Or well, a spell formula you supposedly created once."

"Why not ask your teacher?" Mo Meng said, curiously. "She is, after all, more experienced than me."

Henry snorted. "She said you created a good one, and there's no point recreating it." Before he could interrupt, he added. "Supposedly you popularized it while she was...asleep?"

Code for *trapped and not summoned*. One of the curses of being a jinn, to never be released unless it was willed by another.

"Oh, hmm..." Mo Meng fell silent. "I think I know what she's asking about." Eyes narrowed, he added. "It's about what's happening on the border, isn't it?"

Henry nodded, and touched his chest where a small medallion sat. There were multiple reasons to pass through borders, but even for those who were content to be homebodies, the raids were beginning to affect them. Where the mortal world moved, the supernatural were affected.

After all, though they might have grown in number over the years, as individual species and as a whole, the supernatural were still very much a minority.

EIGHT
Dropped Bait

"Will you help?" Henry asked him, all eager and earnest. Mo Meng remembered what it was like to be that young, in the dim recesses of his memory. Full of energy and enthusiasm, their vision of the world not clouded by hundreds of tragedies, both great and small. By failure and the exhaustion of standing up, over and over again.

"It depends," he replied eventually. "You'd have to tell me what you're planning and showcase what you intend." He looked around, shrugged. "Not here, anyway. Nor can I take too much time off."

"Don't governments have the right to dictate who gets to enter their country?" Kelly asked. "We don't want people who can't pay their way in Canada…" She grimaced. "Our healthcare system is already strained enough."

"Well, that's a provincial matter," Marilyn pointed out. "If we could convince some of those outside the cities to vote for someone other than a Conservative government that wants to privatize the entire system, maybe we'd see an improvement."

"And sort out how people are on-boarded. There's a lot of doctors being delivery drivers," Kelly pointed out. "Had a neighbor who was a surgeon and couldn't afford to take the exams to become a doctor here, even if she was one in India. She never practiced again, because of all that."

"A complete waste," Marilyn sniffed. "It's not like they're going to bleed you without reason these days."

"There's reasons to bleed people?" Henry said, sarcastically.

"Actually, there are," Marilyn said. "Sometimes, the body overproduces and holds onto too much iron. The fastest way to help drain the amount of iron in the body is to force the body to utilize it via bloodletting."

"Should I be surprised that you know that?" Henry said, amused more than anything else.

"Still..." Kelly said doggedly. "Your magic lets people through without checking, makes it possible for people to sneak in. Might they not be the wrong kind?"

Almost in unison, Henry and Mo Meng twitched at those words. Even Marilyn looked a little put off by Kelly's word, making her frown. "What?"

"It's not normally a word we recommend you use, my dear," Marilyn said. "It has a lot of connotations."

"Especially for people like us," Mo Meng said. "You know, I wanted to come to North America in the early part of the twentieth century. See what it was about, but I couldn't."

"Why?"

"I was undesirable, of course. They had a head tax at first, but by the time I was in position to come over, they had blocked all immigration by the Chinese." He shook his head. "It shames me that I left it at that, that I chose to let them choose to do what they wished then. Left those who were trapped here to the tender mercies of a government that cared little for them."

"You ask what happens when magic is released, but do you not realize that such magic is already in- use?" Mo Meng waved a hand around. "The world has not ended. Countries thrive. You speak of a fear of what might be, when 'might be' has already happened."

Kelly ducked her head a little, accepting the point that the world had not ended. Even so, "You still didn't answer the question."

"The question? Are governments allowed to dictate who comes and goes?" Mo Meng frowned. "An interesting philosophical question, truly."

"It's not philosophical, it's practical. People live here and pay taxes, we have a finite resource in our hospitals, in our—"

"If you say land, I'm going to laugh," Henry said.

"—housing. On top of that, there's also people who don't fit..."

"Fit?"

"They bring the wrong kind of beliefs to our country. Things we changed a long time ago. They're trying to pull us backwards. Arranged marriages. Religious law. Caste systems." She sniffed. "They come from places where the patriarchy is even stronger, and they push us backwards. The way some of them treat women, it's disgusting."

"So you'd tar every single individual with the same brush?" Marilyn asked. "All vampires crave the blood of virgins, all dwarves love gold and orcs are bloodthirsty?"

"Wizards are isolated and inscrutable," Mo Meng murmured.

"Well, that one might be true," Marilyn said. "Maybe those views were once true, once a long time ago. But we changed. It wasn't easy, it took a long time, it took people willing to accept, teach and most of all, give us a chance."

Kelly shifted, hunched her shoulders. "But why do we have to do it?"

Mo Meng smiled, tilted his head to the side. "Do you know why I like food?"

"Because you make it tasty?" Henry said with a little smirk.

"I didn't always, you know. It took time and lessons and persistence, much like magic." Mo Meng smiled. "I had to learn, from teachers all over the world, how to be better. Traveled to dozens, hundreds of countries over centuries to learn. I was the stranger then, the person who was in the wrong."

"Some things shouldn't be accepted."

"Perhaps, but a bull in a china shop does little to arrange it," Mo Meng said. "We can only change what we can change, people can only change if we demand it of them. Putting them in a corner offers them little chance to change, because they're never challenged to. We can do our best not to bring in those who are too disruptive, but do you think Henry, myself or those we trust to use the magic would be giving it to those truly 'undesirable'?"

"No...not yet." Then she looked at Henry. "I don't really know him, though."

"Nor do I. Though I know what he did. And Lily trusts him." Mo Meng sighed. "I think, of those seated at this table, he's probably the best person here."

"Even me?"

"By demonstratable actions? Yes." And perhaps there was a little guilt in his assessment. After all, Henry had done what he had not, had sacrificed what many would have considered unimaginable power to do the right thing. He had been willing to make a choice that no one else, not in thousands of years, had been willing to do.

And that, more than anything, was why Mo Meng was willing to speak to the boy.

NINE
The First Dish

Having successfully killed the conversation, Mo Meng sat back with a little smile. Henry was uncomfortable with the attention and praise, the way Kelly was looking at him appraisingly. Looking around anywhere but at her, he eventually coughed into his hand and waved it at their surroundings.

"So, uhh, why are we here?"

"Soft opening for the restaurant," Marilyn replied, leaning forwards. "It's quite the thing, really. They invited all kinds of influencers and critics." She nodded to where a couple of women were trying to discreetly angle their phones so that they could catch the group in their photos. "Smile. You're likely going to be famous."

Henry winced, looking down at his simple jeans and t-shirt combo. No wonder they had not wanted to let him in. He certainly brought down the tone of the restaurant. Running a hand through his hair, he tried to pull it back into some shape and was almost tempted to cast a little glamour.

Whether it was to corrupt or subtly alter the videos or make himself look better, he was still uncertain.

"Isn't that a problem?" Kelly asked Marilyn curiously.

"You mean the old wives' tale about reflections?" When Kelly nodded, Marilyn smiled and shook her head. "Do you know how it came about?"

"No....?"

"Silver. Mirrors were often backed with silver when the rumor started. Because of the way silver interacts with our magic, for some members of our kind, it could remove the glamour and magic we used," Marilyn replied.

"Still does," Mo Meng added. "If you can find pure silver items, that is. Which is rarer these days."

Marilyn inclined her head in acknowledgement. "It never removed us entirely, of course, but many of the older members and some specific lineages had more difficult issues." She gestured to the phones. "Those don't matter. After all, you can see me, can't you? So why shouldn't those?"

Kelly shrugged. "Magic?"

"It doesn't exactly work that way," Henry said. "Magic really is just another force, if you will, that affects current physics. You can move something because you're utilizing some kind of force to move it. Might not look like you're doing anything, but you are. Just like you can't see electricity in the air, or the wind, doesn't mean neither of them are there."

"Right..." Henry could hear the doubt in her voice, and he understood. It was hard to imagine a force that you could neither see, touch or feel, and which was nevertheless all around you. It was only at the edges that you might notice its effects on the world, the way people might turn, sensing another's attention on them. Or the hunch that made you stop, moments before a car came careening around the corner. Flickers of unimaginable luck, magic gathered through years or decades of accidental use till it was ready to be utilized in a single burst of need or will or euphoria.

"So, not to be ungrateful or anything but..." He scratched his cheek. "Do I have to pay for this? Because I didn't really plan for this."

"Still having money problems?" Mo Meng said, amused.

"It's not like the council's exactly paying me properly, you know," Henry grumped. Sure, he got a stipend from the Mage Council, but it was not exactly generous. Especially when you considered everything he had to do and how much travel was involved. All his other work, his responsibilities, and running –after—and paying for—Lily meant he was skint most of the time.

Never mind the small, but regular, amount he put into a savings fund for retirement. A course of action that the older members of the community had insisted he undertake immediately, now that he was part of it and likely to live a few hundred years. If not longer.

Which raised the other question... why some magicians like Mo Meng and Merl lived forever, it seemed, and most others died after a while. No one had given him a proper answer beyond 'lost magic', not even Lily who should know. Then again, maybe it was for the best that such magic stayed lost. Not like the world needed more old, grumpy wizards running around looking to change how things worked; holding onto their beliefs.

"Were you not working as a private investigator before?'

"More like a private cleaner," Henry muttered. "So, about payment..."

Before he could get an answer, one of the waiters glided over. This time, he arrived with multiple stacked plates, held easily in his hands with consummate skill that seemed somewhat like magic. He bowed to the group, placing the appetizer on their table. "The appetizer, ladies and gentlemen."

Henry was not ashamed to admit that he salivated at the sight of the dish before him. It was not large, barely half the size of his hand, but it looked delicious. The base was a rectangular block of golden brown potatoes, cut into thin slices and stacked, while on top was a peeled shrimp, only the head and a small portion of the tail left behind to make it recognizable. The shrimp was perfectly cooked, the black and red color of its cooked skin clearly visible, glistening between the segmented portions of its body. A light purple-red sauce had been drizzled over the bottom portion, and green, orange and white –garnishes—watercress, carrots and ginger or radish—topped the dish to give it further visual appeal.

"Our appetizer for today is a black tiger shrimp served with potato pavé and topped with a reduced pear-plum sauce."

Eyes wide, Henry found himself licking his lips. The presentation was one thing, but the —smell—subtle, but redolent of potatoes roasted in a cream sauce and then fried afterwards—that wafted up from the plate made him smile. He leaned forward, hands touching the utensils before him, and picked up the fork and knife, drawing in a breath. The sauce smelled a touch sweet, the lightest hint of seafood tickling his senses as he breathed in.

First, to make sure he didn't make a mess, he took the prawn off the plate. Cut off the head and the tail, pushing them aside. He debated, for a moment, if it would be rude to suck on the head, then looked up to see Mo Meng smiling at him, almost as though he knew exactly what he was thinking.

He decided that it probably was not done, not in this kind of place. A pity—the brains could often be the best part.

Slice off a portion of the prawn body, noting how easily the knife sliced through the meat. A feature of the knife or the cooking? Hard to tell, but when he cut at the potatoes too, pushing through the many layers, it was just as simple. There was minor resistance, as he encountered what he could only imagine to be charred or crusted portions of potato as he went in. Maybe sugar?

That would be strange, to add sugar on top; but potatoes themselves transformed into sugar, didn't they? when cooked. Or was that fermentation? He could never remember, being more of a takeout and fast food kind of person.

Put the entire thing together, and a quick decision had to be made. Sauce or no sauce?

No sauce to start. He popped the stacked forkful into his mouth, feeling the warmth of the food transfer into his mouth. Not too intense, just a touch of warmth that spread all through his mouth. The potatoes were cream-filled, heavy in his mouth, baked long enough that the top was crunchy and salted to perfection. A heavy, heavenly taste before he tasted the prawn next.

The fresh taste of the sea, the meat firm and giving a little as he chewed on it. Salt from the sea, very sweet and succulent, a taste of wine and alcohol on his tongue. It paired with the heavier cream to give it lightness, the slight crunch of the garnish almost undetectable.

Perfect.

Henry didn't realize he had taken another bite, this time filled with the pear-plum sauce. Surprising that it was not as sweet as he had imagined, but more robust, adding to the contrast in the potatoes and cutting the heaviness of the cream a little.

In four bites, barely enough time to savor it, the appetizer was gone and Henry was looking around, wondering if he could find time to make a few more dollars to come back here. This time on his own dime.

Ten

Tricky Appetizer

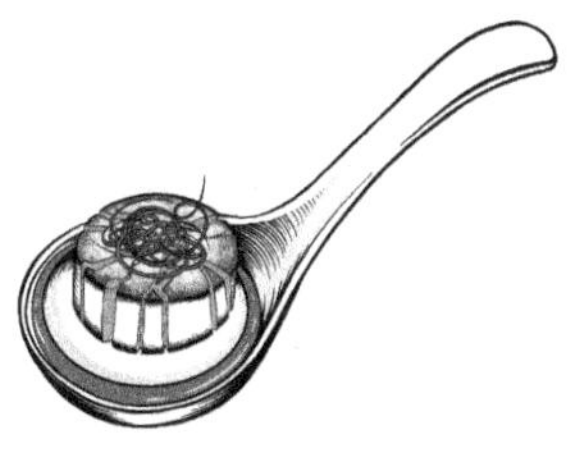

Mo Meng made sure to hide his frown, as he stared down at his plate and then at the newcomer happily chomping away. He pushed aside concerns about magic, about the use of it and the increasingly stringent checks at the border. While there were numerous smuggling operations to get the more difficult to disguise members of their society through such checkpoints, the majority of supernaturals –did—and preferred to—use the 'official' channels.

A problem for another time, for another organization. He would not get involved, other than as a consultant. Not just because he did not want to bother, but because he had no true understanding of the various methods in use. The magic portions, he was certain he could learn quickly enough—and probably would, once Henry was done.

It was the physical side, the mundane methodologies employed. He had heard words thrown around like *face recognition* and *gait identification technology* and *selective screening*, all based on algorithms and AI learning software, and he was, he had to admit, lost.

No, better to let the youngsters work it out, study their magic and then modify it as necessary.

Anyway, it was not as though he had to worry about it. His passport and citizenship were technically still valid, and when the time came, the government would swap it out for another, with more up to date information. All done quietly, without the need to alert other governments, to warn them of the kind of people coming through. Or perhaps, they would—depending on how closely they were allied.

Strange, how the world had changed. Centuries ago, none of that mattered. You could go where you wished, no country barring your way, though local reception was always tricky. The need to manage the flow of travelers was non-existent, as travel was so difficult that only a small number ever did so.

Though, funnily enough, locals might find it harder to move back then. Serfdom, indentured servitude and slavery; the need to tie peasants to farmland created its own kind of restrictions.

Now it was all about usefulness, about productivity and what kind of 'good' an individual could bring. A world that had stopped seeing individuals as people and instead as drains or assets to resources.

It all made Mo Meng tired, really. That was why he had turned back to cooking, to his own enforced retirement. In time, it would pass, or so he hoped. And if not, well... everything passed. Even the greatest empire.

More importantly, he pierced the potatoes, lifted his fork. Noted how the portions of potato came apart, slipped one piece into his mouth and chewed, mouth flooding with cream. Strange, to mix pear and plum into the sauce, to add prawns rather than something more traditional like scallops or something heavier.

Not his first choice, but a good contrast; though...

"Lemon?"

"What?" Marilyn asked.

"Nothing. I was just thinking out loud."

"About adding lemon to this? Or that there was a hint of lemon in the potatoes?" Marilyn stabbed the final portion of potato and swiped it through the sauce before popping the whole thing into her mouth. She chewed slowly, tongue working from side to side, before pronouncing her judgment. "I don't taste any."

"Just what I might do differently," Mo Meng murmured. "I was thinking there was too much sweet and heaviness for my liking. Something lighter might help..."

"Already planning to improve on the chef's recipe?" she said, amused.

"Not improve. This is very good," Mo Meng said, finishing off his own appetizer in moments. "Trying to make it suit my own taste."

"What's the difference? You're still changing it."

"What's the difference between two paintings by a pair of masters?" Mo Meng said. "Chinese painters often took the same motifs, cherry blossoms, bamboo, horses, and did them over and over again. Hundreds, thousands, of the same thing. And yet..."

"There are differences," Kelly said.

"Art is about making the work your own. Cooking and recipes are the same, after a certain point. Sometimes you work with the same ingredients, but you alter it to suit your taste." A slight inclination to the room. "At a certain point, you alter it to the diner's taste, if you know them well enough."

"Do you do that for us?" Marilyn asked

An inclination of the head was answer enough.

"And what do you do for me? Beyond making my meat rarer." A flash of a pointed grin at that, cutting off the obvious answer.

"You like your food bold, with extremes in the flavor profile. I add more spice, more contrast, a touch more salt for you than for others." He quirked a lip. "Well, for most of your kind, really. The change that gave you immortality also decreased the sensitivity of certain taste buds, so it's needed. But you don't enjoy spice as much as others, so I'm more careful with that. You prefer a little texture, too, so I sometimes let the food char further."

Marilyn's lips turned upwards. "Rare for a man to pay so much attention. It's quite flattering."

Instead of rising to the bait, he gave her an unimpressed look. "You know I do that for all my customers. At least, as much as I can." He gestured to the room, to the way the kitchen was blocked off. "This kind of set-up doesn't let you pay attention to the individual. It focuses on the perfection of each dish as envisioned by the chef, a replication of the same dish over and over again with no variation."

"You don't sound impressed," Henry said.

"It tries to turn an art form into a factory production. Takes the wonder out of cooking, puts the pressure all on the cook to reproduce the same thing over and over again. Chasing perfection."

"Isn't that what the Japanese do, though?" Kelly said. "When they make rice, they take years to learn how to do it properly. And then more years learning how to cut fish, how to roll sushi and make it perfect."

"It is," Mo Meng acknowledged her point. "There's nothing wrong with that, really. Almost necessary, to become a master. You chase excellence, perfection if you will, knowing that it will never be possible." He shrugged. "But it can also grind you down, if you cannot find the joy in it as well."

Kelly nodded, turning her head to look at the waiters. They all looked serious and polished, perfect in their starched shirts and pressed pants, always attentive, always unobtrusive. She reflected on the noise in the room, how it was both too loud for her liking, and also a touch too quiet.

There was none of the boisterous talk that filled the Nameless Restaurant on a daily basis. The laughter and the occasional startled cry of surprise or delight at a meal, or good news passed on. Here, the conversation consisted of serious businessmen and self-obsessed influencers, taking photos and setting up ring lights so that they could properly document every moment.

Near the front, there were a couple standing, posing for photos as the hostess took dozens of shots, moving through various angles to ensure they had the perfect addition to their socials. The restaurant name was illuminated in LED lights, the cool oval ring highlighting the entrance, ferns and flowers in each corner to add a pop.

A fabulous life, or so it seemed on the outside. If the couple hadn't been there for five minutes now, taking photo after photo to get it just right.

"We should add some alcohol," Kelly decided, looking right at Mo Meng as she spoke. Challenging him to gainsay her on this.

Eleven

Alcohol & Drinks

"Alcohol?" Mo Meng blinked, almost spoke, only to find the words had drawn a waiter over.

"Would the sirs or madam like to see the wine list?" the waiter said stiffly. "Or I may request the sommelier to come over and make recommendations."

Mo Meng cut his gaze over to Marilyn at that. While he had some experience with wine and alcohol in general, there were degrees of expertise involved. While the vampire might not have the subtle taste buds of her yesteryear, he also knew she was just as likely to have studied the process. On top of that, while her tastebuds might have deadened, her sense of smell had improved, like most predators.

"No need to request. Just have them send over the bottle that's most suitable," Marilyn said. "We should really have had one for the appetizer."

"My apologies, madam. That was my fault. I should have checked," the waiter said, offering a slight bow as he spoke.

"It's fine, this one caused quite the ruckus. I would have forgotten too," Marilyn said, looking at Henry who shrugged unrepentantly.

"It must be hard," Kelly muttered, looking around at the waiters and the older man who had served them, drawn away to a corner where he was being talked to. Nothing as flagrant as shouting or gesticulating, but if you knew what to look for, you could tell he was being dressed down.

Mo Meng debated saying something, then left it. Instead, he looked at his employee, curious if she would elaborate.

"Just having to be perfect all the time. That's what this place runs on, isn't it? Perfection?" she said. "I mean, you do it, of course. In the kitchen. Your dishes are all very good, near perfect each time they come out."

"Near perfect?" he said to tease her.

"Yes. Perfection isn't possible, right? There's always something wrong, if you look closely." She sighed. "But I also know you try to do the best you can, and I know you also fail a lot. They just never see it."

"They?" Marilyn sniffed. "I'll let you know, I've tasted more of his failures than you have."

Kelly made a noise in her throat at that, looking at Mo Meng, who shrugged. "We've known each other a long time. And the restaurant's just the latest in a variety of places I've cooked." He could not help but smile in fond remembrance of cooking fires, borrowed hearths in open villas in Italy, and the low-baked coals in the Middle East. Good times, a long time ago.

"You think he was good, but really, he was just okay." She gestured to the kitchen. "When we first met, he could cook serviceable meals but nothing spectacular."

"I was working in a merchant caravan," Mo Meng said, mildly. "It wasn't as though I had a lot of spices or other ingredients to work with."

"Serviceable," she repeated. "But he got better, with practice. Got as good as these people." A nod towards the kitchen. "And then, well, he still had time, so he went through his experimental stage."

"It wasn't a stage."

"Oh, it really was." Marilyn leaned in, faux-whispered. "He tried things he knew weren't going to work. Wasted food—and then insisted on eating a good portion of it, because otherwise 'how would he know' he would say." She shuddered. "I made sure not to visit him often back then."

"How long did it last?" Henry asked, curiously.

"Most of the seventeenth century?" Marilyn shrugged. "Something like that."

"It was an exciting time. Spices were much easier to acquire," Mo Meng replied. "A lot of trade flowed into Europe, and there were new spices and dishes coming in all the time. The recipes that many cultures used were transitioning too. It was a good time to be a chef."

"Weren't potatoes coming into fashion then?" Marilyn muttered.

"They arrived during that period, but not many people were putting them into their food. Mostly used for pig slop, actually. Or for their flowers."

"Oh, yes. Marie Antoinette wore them once, didn't she? Set the whole court and French noble courts ablaze." The old vampire shook her head. "For a time, people were raiding peasant farms for the flowers, destroying the potatoes themselves."

"Mmm, yes. It took a century or two for the plant to become so dominant. Famine and the needs of the sea made the difference."

"The sea?" Now Henry was curious, leaning forwards. "What's the sea have to do with potatoes?"

"Scurvy, of course." Seeing the blank look on the mage's face, Mo Meng sighed. "They don't really teach you anything, do they?"

"I know about scurvy," Henry protested. "That's what lemons and oranges are for, no? They used to bring barrels of them."

"Or potatoes. There's a lot of vitamin C in potatoes—though they didn't know that was what was going on. It was more an unhappy accident." At the looks Kelly and Henry gave him, Mo Meng clarified. "The Spaniards only fed potatoes to some of the Incan slaves who worked their mines. When they didn't die of scurvy...." He shrugged. "Well, even they could work that one out."

"So they started carrying potatoes?" Henry said, shocked.

"Yes. South America was where it originally happened." Mo Meng smiled tightly. "And yes, they really did. The old histories got it wrong."

"Oh." Kelly frowned. "So the potato went from pig food to high cuisine..." She recalled the dish they had just been served, how carefully it had been prepared. She smiled a little, in amusement.

"Happens that way quite often. Just like lobster," Mo Meng murmured.

"I still don't really care for it. The rat of the ocean..." Marilyn shuddered.

"Many of those from your age don't." Mo Meng smirked. "I've never seen the problem with it."

"You wouldn't."

He chuckled at the accusation, while Kelly watched the pair bat answers back and forth and wondered. Rather than let them continue, though, she asked for clarification. "So you saw all these spices, tomatoes and potatoes and the like, come over? And tested them out yourself?"

"I did." Mo Meng smiled, tightly. "Spent most of my time in North Africa during that period, with occasional sojourns in southern Europe. The environment further south was better for me back then."

"Because it was warmer?" Kelly asked.

Marilyn suddenly broke out laughing, and Mo Meng sighed, looking at the woman. It took a little while before she calmed down, waving at Kelly as she answered.

"It's just that I remembered why you weren't in Europe then."

The look Mo Meng shot her made Marilyn grin, but she mimed zipping her mouth shut. When Henry started to ask, Mo Meng sent him a death glare too, and remembering his own needs, the mage subsided. It was only Kelly who plotted to get that story out of the vampire at some point. Though from the look that Mo Meng offered her, he was sure to find out.

Still, before they could continue their conversation, the next dish arrived.

TWELVE
Main Arrival

F our dishes. That was the common number in these modern times, where dishes were often larger than they needed to be to feed your average diner. In truth, the size of dishes was tiny, compared to when people worked on farms or spent all day on their feet. However, for your average worker, it was often too much.

And that was in Canada, where portion sizes were big but not ridiculous. The US leaned towards serving enough to feed two or three individuals from a single entree. Though, with the recent inflation in prices, portion sizes were shrinking a little with each passing month as restaurants strove to survive.

Funny, how the business changed over time.

Once eating out was common, a necessity in cities, where having the space or time to cook one's own food, or proper ventilation or even a large enough fire, was a luxury. Rural life was different, of course, with meals made by women along with the rest of their housework, but in cities, in the last few centuries, it was all about expedience when individuals worked two, three, sometimes even four jobs before they crashed back into bed.

Sleeping in shifts was not uncommon for the poorest, individuals utilizing the same bed and rarely even having time to wash up before it was time to rise again for their next job. Eating food from roadside vendors, easy to consume buns or pies or other, handheld meals was not uncommon. For a time, that was life; until unions and gangs fought for better working conditions and the hold of the nobles and rich was broken.

After that, dining out faded a little, as the luxury of eating at home, at having time to eat at home, increased. Diners for roadside carriages or truckers continued to thrive, of course, inns for those who needed a place to sleep and eat; but simple restaurants with sit-down meals for your everyday person were more uncommon, a rare treat to be enjoyed when possible.

Perhaps once a week, perhaps a little more often if you were rich.

Then came the wars and the time of abundance after that, and soon enough, restaurants thrived and eating out was not just uncommon but expected. The world swung back to long hours, luxury becoming everyday, time once more at a premium for some.

Now, though, as prices began to rise, the simple joy of consuming another's meal, of relaxing, was beginning to disappear. Too many restaurants, too high costs, too few willing or able to pay the price. The entire economy was shifting once more, and Mo Meng wondered how the world would change again.

Of course, for a place like this, that catered to the elite—perhaps very little. The rich always found a way to pay for their desires, and never concerned themselves with the needs of those below. Catering to those above generally went well—if you had the skill to back it up.

And if there wasn't a minor revolution brewing. Sometimes, being too closely related to those above might be hazardous to one's existence.

Four dishes: palate cleanser, appetizer, main, and then, of course, a dessert. In a place like this, perhaps a second palate cleanser might be offered, so that the dessert might be tasted without additional taste.

Mo Meng sighed, as the meal arrived. There had been three choices at the beginning: a pasta, a seafood, and a vegetarian option for those who did not consume either.

Dishes were served quickly and smoothly, even Henry having had a chance earlier to dictate his choice of dish. Mo Meng knew how much of a scramble that would have been, to get the dish added to the pile so that it would come out at the same time as everyone else's.

"For the lady, a mushroom, bacon and scallop carbonara. As always, the pasta was made in-house just this morning by our pasta chef. There are three types of mushrooms: morels, wild oyster mushrooms and maisutake mushrooms alongside PEI scallops. The bacon is cured and smoked in-house, supplied by a local wild boar farm a bare hundred and twenty kilometers from here. We have added organic shallots from a local farm, the PEI scallops were farmed and flash frozen before being delivered within twenty-four hours, and all of it topped by a thirty-six month aged

Parmigiano-Reggiano." The pasta dish was placed before Kelly, the smell of egg yolk, parmesan and bacon wafting into the air as it was set in front of her and causing her to smile.

Not the most adventurous or stunning dish, but a crowd favorite and a safe bet. Mo Meng tilted his head around, noting who was consuming it or not, and had to admit it was not a bad choice. Many of the social media influencers had gone for it, the sprinkle of green onions, the dash of dark bacon meat and most of all, the lack of novelty drawing many to order it rather than try something unusual.

Like a vegetarian or seafood dish.

"For the gentleman and lady, the curried basa on jasmine rice. The basa fish was purchased from a local fishing co-op in Indonesia, the water and soil tested regularly to ensure minimal contamination." Mo Meng's eyebrows rose a little at those words, though he was surprised to note that Marilyn was nodding along happily. "The curry sauce is a light coconut sauce, the curry the chef's own variation on a Thai recipe with fresh vegetables and garnishing. The rice was imported from a small farm in Cambodia that has an exclusive arrangement with the restaurant at this time."

"Seems a little much, no?" Mo Meng muttered. Having a single customer never seemed like a good option to him; it made one dependent. Then again, if the restaurant was committing to buying all the rice at one go, whenever it came out—and most rice could be harvested two to three times a year—it might be a decent boost in income.

Still, for all his reservations, the dish itself looked quite appetizing. Unlike the usual red or lurid heavy oranges and flame color of most curries, the basa fish was pale and creamy. Mo Meng could smell just the lightest hint of the curry spices and chili in it, but guessed that it would be a somewhat milder spice blend than he would have preferred himself. On the other hand, the pile of rice served next to it was formed into a bowl, with a small compression right in the center to allow gravy to be spooned into it. A garnish of orange carrots, yellow and red peppers and green scallions placed over the fish and his rice added to the artful arrangement.

Ignoring Mo Meng's low muttered comment, the waiter took the last plate from the other waiting waiter and placed it before Henry.

"And finally, our fried cauliflower steak with cashew gravy, seasoned breadcrumbs and a herb and ginger relish. We source the majority of our ingredients from local farms in Canada, with the cashews from Central America."

Of all the dishes, the cauliflower was the darkest by far. Deep fried with breadcrumbs, taken out and then smothered with a dark gravy and vibrant green relish, a second set of dipping sauces added to the side. In comparison to the other two, it was a vibrant, almost juicy contrast, with the deep smell of the creamy cashew gravy and the fresh herb relish reaching upwards and yanking attention.

Not what you would expect from a vegetarian dish, and Mo Meng was actively curious how that might taste. He might just have to try a small portion later, though he was not—technically—working today. Thus his own choice of a dish he knew would certainly be good.

After all, the base recipe was one that he had taught the other.

Thirteen

A Meatless Objection

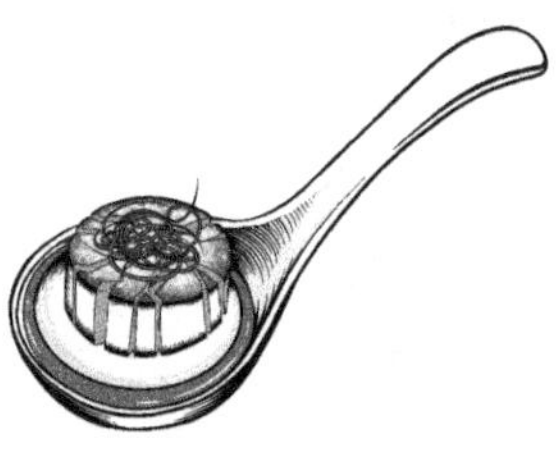

Henry had to admit, he was eyeing the rest of the dinners with interest. He had considered ordering something like the carbonara; it was easy and safe and he knew what it probably tasted like. However, having something heavy like pasta in his stomach would likely put him right to sleep, and that was not a viable option considering he would have to speak with the Grand Magus later.

Or Magician? He really could not remember the terms. The Mage Council had quite a number, and while he technically was part of the council these days, the truth was that he acted more in his old role as an independent contractor than connected with the council itself.

Not that they had many direct reports—it wasn't as though they were trying to control all magic, just the use of it. Which was why only their enforcers, their council members and a few administrative staff were directly hired. Everyone else received grants or stipends if they were researchers, or just kept their head down, intent on not being caught out.

Of course, the number of malcontents and troublemakers was remarkably low. For the most part, idle troublemakers just were not very good at becoming mages. It required a combination of focus, discipline and talent to be even mildly competent at magic.

Well, unless you received an early cheat the way Henry had. But not everyone was lucky enough to obtain a magic ring with an all-powerful genie in it, after all.

"Never took you to be a vegetarian," Kelly said, frowning. "You didn't order that way the last time you visited."

"Just trying something new." He smiled at Kelly, noticing again how cute the waitress was. Not that it mattered, beyond idle appreciation. Relationships were... Well. Complicated. No one wanted a boyfriend that was out of town for three-quarters of a month, or even more. "Anyway, nothing wrong with eating healthy once in a while."

"Nothing says that vegetarian food is healthier than other kinds." Mo Meng pointed to Henry's dish. "Deep fried food, no matter what the base is, is not particularly healthy; no?"

"Less calories, I would think. Than a big hunk of meat."

"Protein is necessary, though."

"Which is why it's good they have potatoes here too," Henry said. "And it's not like I'm lifting rocks, so I don't really need that much." He tried for a smile. "I'm more of a thinker, you know."

"Magic use requires a lot of calories, though, if you're casting regularly." Mo Meng frowned. "If you're not eating well..."

"Do I look that unhealthy to you?" Henry said as a rejoinder. When the others gave him a once over, the girls doing it more thoroughly than Mo Meng in a way that made him blush a little, he coughed. "I do fine. I know better than to neglect my health. And I do work out, a bit."

"Oh?" Kelly said. "The gym?"

"Don't have time to go to them, mostly. I prefer calisthenics," Henry said. "If necessary, there are a few spells I can use that increase the weight on my body, which makes it a harder workout and adds to the effort."

"Oh! That's smart. Why don't more people do that?" Kelly said.

"It's not, if you have a heart problem." Mo Meng's lips thinned. "Or a clot. Or any other of a half-dozen ailments that putting higher gravitational stress on your whole body, including blood vessels and lungs, can worsen."

"I don't crank it up that much," Henry complained. "And I'm perfectly healthy. We checked."

"We?"

"Lily and, umm, a few others." Henry scratched the side of his neck. "I had a few encounters that ended with me in a hospital, and a few others where physicals were required after the fact."

Kelly's eyes widened as Mo Meng frowned. "Borer worms?"

"Once. Then there was a wendigo that they thought had caught me."

That brought a hiss from Marilyn while Mo Meng frowned. "I thought we eradicated most of those."

"There are a few left, but this time it was a case of mistaken identity. Just an over-active fae doppelganger."

Mo Meng relaxed while Kelly looked back and forth between the group, confused. Rather than answer her, even as rather unpleasant memories returned of being forced to stand around naked but for a very thick layer of mud and leaves, Henry turned his attention to his meal.

Deep fried cauliflower steak. Henry was rather intrigued. Cutting into a cauliflower steak was, obviously, not the same as cutting into an actual steak. It did not have the same resistance, the toughness one would expect from meat. In fact, using the beautifully weighted steak knives provided seemed like overkill. In moments, he had a piece separated and he was mopping up the brown and green sauces to coat the breadcrumb-covered, pale, fried cauliflower to slip into his mouth.

He hesitated before slipping the portion into his mouth, the rich smell of the gravy, undercut by hints of fat and oil along with the fresh herbs, reaching upwards. Deep fried breadcrumbs and the slightly bitter smell of the cauliflower was rather pleasant, and reminiscent of the steak it purported to mimic, though different too.

Probably for the best.

He popped the entire mouthful into his mouth before the gravy dripped. The moment it touched his tongue, new tastes burst into life. Salt and pepper, of course, because what good recipe from the west missed out on those? The thick gravy full of rich umami, the zing of fresh herbs that he would swear included mint, thyme and basil. Peppers too, for sure—and not the red or green peppers so loved over here, but something from further south—the Caribbean, he would have sworn. It added a little kick to the herbs, but not so much as to overwhelm the other tastes.

Fried cauliflower had a little more crunch than a piece of beef would have. It was pleasant, just firm enough to have a good texture, but a little more brittle than beef. It came apart as Henry masticated the piece, enjoying the flood of juices that mixed in his mouth.

It was not steak, though it might mimic it in appearance. However, that was fine with Henry. Food that just tried to mimic meat without delving into what made the ingredients unique always seemed a little silly.

After all, if he wanted steak, he could order it.

Beside the cauliflower steak was the starch, the potatoes. A small dollop, no bigger than an ice cream scoop-sized amount of mashed potatoes. Smooth and creamy, with a surprising nutty aftertaste. Scooping up a portion and dipping it in the gravy made him smile a little, though he puzzled over the nutty taste.

"Something wrong?" Mo Meng asked.

"It tastes a little nutty." Henry poked at the mashed potatoes. "Not bad, just...different."

"Probably almond milk rather than cow's milk or cream," Mo Meng explained.

"Oh. That... huh." Henry frowned. "Why?"

"It makes it vegan!" Kelly said, excitedly.

"Why do you care?"

"I don't, but we have a number of customers who do." She looked wide-eyed at Mo Meng, who shrugged.

"It's possible, but it changes the texture a little. You need to add more to it, I find. Roasted garlic helps cover the taste and mixes well. Pepper and paprika can help, and if they're up to it, chili flakes."

"Oooh..." Kelly said enthusiastically.

Henry nodded absently, poked at his food again and switched to the vegetables. Nothing special here—the steamed vegetables were tasty and fresh and there was enough salt and what he assumed was butter—or the vegan equivalent—but it was generally, well, vegetables. They had apparently waved them over a charcoal grill, so at least the steamed vegetables had added crunch and burnt bits. An interesting addition to the dish.

"So...?" Kelly asked, making Henry swallow his latest mouthful. "What do you think?"

"Good. It's good, maybe not the most filling but good."

"Let me try!" She waved hands and utensils over her plate like an eager child, and he could not help but return her enthusiasm. He pushed his plate over, ignoring the bemused looks that his other companions shot the two of them.

Fourteen
Plain and Tasty

Kelly enthusiastically chowed down on the stolen cauliflower steak. It was, as Henry said, good; though for her the almond milk mashed potatoes were the clear winner. Among other things, she had switched to almond milk herself at home, so it was something she could recreate more easily. She made a mental note to try it with chili flakes and some roasted garlic, to give it a little more variety, but it was still a pleasure to eat.

"Here." Reluctantly she handed over some of her own dish to the intriguing mage. She had not seen him for a while, not since his rather dramatic entrance with Lily. Ever since their arrival, her routine—if you could call waitressing at a magical restaurant routine—had been disrupted. More and more interesting mages had arrived, business had grown and with it, her responsibilities.

She could not help but think it had something to do with those two. Which made him interesting and a little mysterious, especially with the hints of the things he was doing. Building magical artifacts to let supernaturals slip through the borders?

Even if she wasn't sure about the exact ethics of that, it was clear that he was. It wasn't as though she told her college friends about the customers she served. Not just because they might not believe her, but also, there was a reason this world was hidden.

For the most part.

"'Tis good!" he muttered, eyes wide as he finished chewing on the twirled pasta she had deposited on his plate.

"It is, isn't it?" she grinned. "You didn't even have the best part."

"The scallops?"

"Mmmhmmm…" She stabbed a mid-sized scallop with her fork, raising it to her mouth and biting in. Fresh and rich, perfectly cooked but smaller than the large ones that had started the meal. A good thing, since it meant that it was a perfect bite size.

The delicate flesh of the scallops split apart into tiny strips, the meat squishing and releasing the taste of ocean water into her mouth, a touch of butter and the richness of the bacon fat it had been cooked and mixed into.

She twirled the carbonara with her fork, utilizing the knife to help bring the rest of the strands together. A small column formed, flaked with bits of wild boar bacon and clear, chopped shallots amidst the glistening pasta, cheese flakes long melted.

When she popped the bite into her mouth, she could not help but close her eyes. Some people criticized buying pasta in restaurants, noting how easy it was to make such dishes at home. To them, Kelly might say that you could buy and cook pork chops or steaks at home too, saving yourself significantly more money.

On the other hand, here was a dish that had wild boar bacon in it—something that was uncommon at best, if not extremely difficult to obtain for most. Wild boar was, in truth, her favorite version of pork.

After all, most pork you could purchase was mass produced, the creatures fed and grown as quickly as possible with the cheapest sources of feed. Most had too much fat, having never had enough chance to move around, and lacked a robustness to their flavor.

Wild boar was raised by smaller farmers for the most part, which meant the animals were generally better cared for. Their growth took time, their feed was more varied, and they were given more space. The farmers knew they could charge more than the factory farms, that their clientele paid a premium for quality.

On top of that, of course, was how the meat was just richer. Porkier, if that was a word, which Kelly was uncertain of. When it came to something like bacon, cold cured with what she assumed was honey or maple syrup, the flavor was both sweet and dense.

Mixed with the sharp tang of good cheese and the shallots, and she could not help but smile as she bit into the pasta. Even the carbonara was better, denser and more flavorful. Most store-bought pasta had very little egg in it, companies cutting costs as much as possible, so that it barely had any flavor or proper texture.

This was house made, fresh and never dried. Made every day, still fresh and flexible, no hard portions from undercooking, and then cooked further in the same pasta water and egg white after everything had blended, so that the flavors penetrated the pasta too.

And the cheese, oh the cheese. Sharp and aged and lovely. She bought parmesan at home, but most of it was cheap; easy to access and with very little taste even when you slathered it on. This was so much better, and when added in the right proportions, it enhanced the entire dish.

On top of that, how many people were likely to buy more than one type of mushrooms—if they even bothered? Certainly not three, pre-cooked properly to extract all the oils and then slathered with butter to absorb, and then, and only then, mixed in with the main pasta dish. Crimini, oyster and shiitake would be her guess, though she would not have bet on it. Maybe truffle, though that might make the dish too expensive.

She considered asking, but that would mean she'd have to stop eating, and well...

"Good, then?" Henry said, amused.

"We should do an Italian night!" Kelly said instead, looking at Mo Meng. "With carbonara and spaghetti and meatballs and lasagna and...!"

"Do you only know pasta dishes for Italian food?" Marilyn said, amused.

"No, there's pizza!"

"With pineapple and tomato sauce?"

Ignoring the hint of humor in Marilyn's voice, Kelly nodded firmly. "Yes! We could have a variety of different pizza toppings. Maybe we could get a list!"

"You know that pineapple and even tomatoes aren't actually traditional in Italian cooking, right?" Henry said slowly.

"What? What do you mean?"

"Italian pizza didn't actually have a tomato base, not until it came to the US."

"No... You're wrong," she protested. "How do you know?"

"Saw it on a video reel, one of those history of cooking ones that they do," Henry said.

"So you believe that?" she said, eyes narrowing.

"Why would they lie?"

The look she gave him made him duck his head. Not content with just looks, she added, "Do you trust everything you read or watch?"

"Of course not! Especially not when it's important."

The pair began to bicker good-naturedly about what was important, forgetting about the other two at the table.

FIFTEEN

A Little Fishy

Marilyn hid a small smile, noting the pair. She turned her head a little, caught Mo Meng's gaze and raised a single eyebrow. He—the too-serious fool that he was—just shook his head, dismissing her concerns and causing her to smirk a bit.

Well, it was probably best not to interfere with young ... lust? Attraction and interest, at least.

In truth, she was grateful to see the waitress being interested in someone a little more age appropriate. While she had little concern about the mage taking an interest in the younger woman, a one-sided crush could be just as devastating to the restaurant as anything else. She had noticed glimmers of it early on, though it had faded as Kelly had gotten to know the older man.

Possibly as she was introduced to the idea of just how old he truly was. It was certainly likely that had decreased her overall interest.

It was tough, in truth, for those who had lived a couple of centuries. Not just older mannerisms—and she had to admit, mortals and mages had it easier than the undead as physical biology altered their mindset more quickly—just weariness with the entire dance.

Not that Mo Meng had any children as far as she knew. Not like some of the other old horndogs who littered the hidden world, with their multiple wives and great-grandchildren. Nor was he entirely an ascetic—she knew he'd had his dalliances over the course of time—but querying him had only brought forth a single comment about fertility spells and a tired smile.

Too tired, so weary and all-knowing that she had not pressed.

They all had their own ghosts, corpses long buried but memories of the past following them into the present. Loved ones and hated enemies, restless spirits that haunted lonely living rooms in penthouse condominiums, teeth reflecting in yellow light, clad in woolen coats and white wigs; whispering broken promises of love everlasting.

"Dish not to your liking?" Mo Meng asked, an eyebrow raised.

She blinked, realized she had frozen, utensils hovering motionless over her plate. Marilyn blinked, consciously, knowing that it was likely she had been staring unblinking into her surroundings for however long she had been lost. Sometimes it could be an hour...

"It's...fine." She licked her lips, running over the slight glossiness of her lipstick. Touched a tongue to a canine, felt it pierce to wake herself up. Tasted blood—old and all too quickly gone—and roused herself further. The hunger came too, as she stared into too-knowing hazel eyes.

"I'm a little insulted..." Mo Meng sniffed.

"You? You're not the cook. For once."

"My recipe. Or, well, close to it." He touched the dish before him, split off a portion of the fillet and spooned it onto the plate of rice. "I serve the full fish, family style with bowls for the rice. Not plates, like here..."

"Individual plates, that's the way they like it here." A twisted smile as she continued. "I hear it's better for the restaurant?"

"More chance of getting a star, at least."

Did she hear a trace of desire in there? Or resentment? No. Probably not. She somehow doubted the old man desired such external forms of validation. He knew better, after all, than to weigh his ego against the fickle taste of the masses.

"Well, it's good." She spooned up some rice already mixed with the light curry sauce and brought it to her lips. Slipped it in and felt the burst of heat—not much, just a touch of spice to give it the necessary 'bite'. A light curry sauce, more yellow with the peppers and onions, than the vibrant red of other curries. Not hot, but a subtle mixture of a half-dozen or more spices.

Funny how curry was always different—every cook making their own paste of powders. Mixing and altering the contents to reach the taste profile they wanted, and yet, each curry undoubtedly from the same family. Recognizable, different but with specifics that marked the curry's origin in one region or another.

Here, lemongrass was the largest signifier of the recipe's southeast Asian origin. The slightly sweet-sour taste of the lemongrass brought the more turmeric-heavy based curry into profile, a small addition of star anise highlighting the cumin and coriander in the dish.

There were other spices in here, though she could not identify them—even her greater ability to pick out individual notes ran into the barrier of ignorance. She could have spent some time learning how to taste and recognize all the notes in the dish, but really, why would she?

Sometimes, it was better to just enjoy a dish for what it was, rather than try to pick it apart. In this case, the rice—jasmine for certain with its fragrant odor—mixed well with the curry sauce. She chewed, swallowed, smiled even as the taste did little to assuage that other hunger.

"What do you think? About what they've done to your recipe?" she asked, then added, "What did they do?"

"Altered the spice blends a little. Brought the spice level down—you know I prefer mine to be hotter." The old man grimaced. "Always hard, of course, balancing the heat levels to customers."

"How would you do that?" Henry spoke up, breaking off from his argument. "Because I do like eating a little spicier than most."

"Chili oils can be a useful addition," Mo Meng replied. "Or fresh chilis, depending on the dish." He frowned at the plate of fish before him. "I'd probably go with fresh chilis here, in fact, quickly toasted, if someone wanted a secondary accompaniment to make it spicier." Then another shrug. "Hotter would help balance some of the spices better, though."

"You don't think it's well balanced?" she asked, noting how one of the nearby waiters stirred, overhearing the words.

Mo Meng shifted, perhaps realizing what he'd said. He shook his head, "Not the way I would cook it, perhaps. He's come up with his own style for the dish, which is appropriate, really." A slight smile then, this one genuine. "It's good he's found his style."

A quick stab of the bok choy and she added it to the next bite, chewing on the vegetable. Marilyn had to admit, it was not to her taste. This vegetable was always a little bitter to her tongue, though less so in the modern day than in the past. Much like brussels sprouts, which had once been intensely bitter before a new strain had been found. Poor people's food, those sprouts, before the change.

The two mages started talking about style, somehow managing to segue the conversation into magical styles. She tuned it out, having little interest in the topic. After all, she could not wield magic—a disadvantage of an undead body, which caused magic to flow in entirely different ways.

Probably for the best, considering the kind of damage they could do if some of her past associates had access to magic. Undeath didn't make individuals evil, but boredom? Oh yes, that truly was the devil's tool.

"Why basa, though?" she asked instead, tired of listening to them talk, as she split apart the fillet with a fork and spooned it into her mouth. Not that she had a problem with the taste; the white fish was sweetish and flakey, perfect for taking on the sauce while holding onto the freshwater taste of the fish. Not the cleanest fish, of course, but not a bottom feeder like catfish.

"White fish," Mo Meng replied, and echoed her thoughts. "Subtle in flavor, not too oily or muddy. Cheap as well, and it's not as sharply recognizable to many as halibut or cod."

"That's important?"

"It is when you want to mix it with a curry." He scooped up another portion for himself. "If you used salmon here, it'd change the taste profile entirely. Waste of the salmon, really. I've made fish head curry with salmon; it's not bad, but it's a little oily and a little, well, too salmon-like. Better to use whitefish, or for fish head curry at least, a catfish head."

"Catfish?" Henry said, surprised. "Not that I don't like it, but…"

"It's fine. There's not as much flesh in the head, so you can use bigger fish. At the same time, you can go a little stronger with the curry then and mute the muddiness." Mo Meng smiled a little. "A little like spell casting, really. You have to balance the inputs. If you're using a less pristine source, you either want the output to suit the necessity or balance it with something that draws out the impurities."

"Like metal mana?"

Marilyn's eyes narrowed and then, catching Kelly's exasperated gaze, she sighed. Well, she had tried to get them off the magic talk.

Sixteen

A Familiar Dish

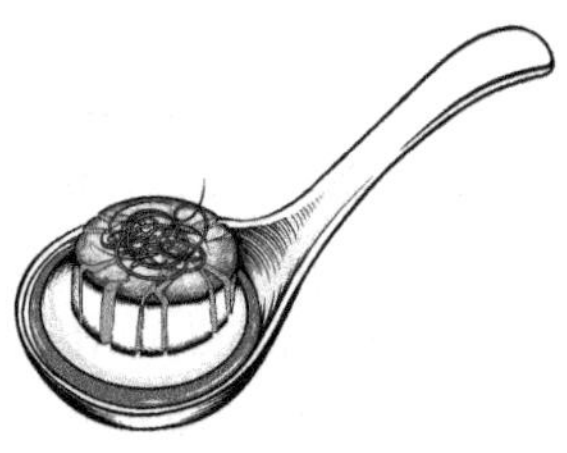

Mo Meng smiled, his head cocked to the side as he listened to the younger mage speak. It was curious, how the pair of them thought. So similar in some ways—they had some of the same teachers—but also different. Lily had been a major factor in Henry's studies, but for a creature who had lived so long, she had a somewhat eclectic view of magic.

"Balancing aspects of spells..." Henry sighed. "I guess you're not wrong. It took me a long time to realize how the formulas interacted, and how to adjust them while casting."

"Formulas?" Mo Meng lips twitched. "She had you go back to Assyrian spell formulas?"

"Some Babylonian too, I think." Henry frowned. "It's bit of a mix, but the spells she inserted are quite varied. Clean, and based off her own spell incantations."

"Oh, she's still using those?" Mo Meng smiled a little, splitting off a portion of fish. He had noted how his piece was almost perfectly cooked, if a touch too long in the oven. Perhaps just too long under the warming lamps; it could be difficult to balance the arrival of dishes, especially on opening night.

He had not complained, for the curry was good. A little sweeter than his own preference—he could have sworn there was tomato or perhaps pineapple in there—but well balanced. It would go over well with most of the clientele they were trying to draw.

Even as the man was confirming his earlier question, explaining a little about how Lily was now working to translate many of the older spells into her 'simplified' spell formula, something bothered him about Henry's answer. It took him a moment to realize what it was.

"...and there's of course, the paint magic of—"

"She inserted spells into your mind?" Mo Meng blurted out, surprised.

"Well... yes." Henry frowned, then brightened in sudden realization. "Oh, you don't know the story."

"What story?"

"I... well. I found her and one of my early wishes was to learn magic. To do that, she inserted spells into my mind like uhhh..." He frowned, then ducked his head. "Well, like a video game. Hit the button, feed in Mana and away it goes."

Mo Meng relaxed a little. "Well, memorizing spell formulas was always hard. Impressing such magic can be a shortcut..." He trailed off as he saw Henry shaking his head.

"No, no." Henry frowned. "It's not like... uhh..." He looked down at the food on his plate and smiled. "Like, magic formulas and spells are like recipes, right? Once you learn them, you can manipulate the recipes and alter the ingredients. Just like you said."

"Yes..."

"What she did was the equivalent of ummm... boxed cakes. Prepackaged all the ingredients of a spell and blended it in and then I just had to add the 'wet' ingredients to make it work. Mana and will, and boom, spell."

"You can do that?" Kelly said, excited.

"No."

"Yes."

Mo Meng and Henry stared at one another, before Mo Meng inclined his head to Henry to explain. He, in turn, looked at Kelly.

"You can, if you're Lily. She's..."

"Irresponsible." Mo Meng scowled. "Magic should not just be gifted like that. It's dangerous—for the recipient and the caster. There is a reason we teach apprentices slowly and make them learn patience. There are many ways of building up an individual's control and their body's ability to manage qi."

"Qi?" Kelly frowned.

"Energy—internal or external. I prefer it to other terms for it, like fate or god's blood or—"

"Mana," Henry interjected.

"That's from World of Warcraft!" Kelly said.

"Yes, and other games. It's what I use on my screens."

"Your screens..." Mo Meng looked at the man, who then had to explain how he had created a game screen to help him with his casting, a way to manage his resource collection and a number of active spells. He seemed so enthusiastic about it that Mo Meng chose to just nod his head in acknowledgement, though it felt like a lot of work to accomplish what you could do intuitively with enough training.

"It's efficient, really. It's probably the spell I use the most," Henry was explaining to Kelly. "It's also quite problematic, and inaccurate. Lily showed me how to make it, but she didn't give me the spells that time, just made me learn it from the beginning." He let out a gusty sigh. "Said I'd do better if I studied something I was actually interested in."

"So can anyone learn magic?" Kelly said, curiously.

Mo Meng frowned, though he wiped the frown away in moments. Keeping his head down, he ignored the discussion as he scooped up some rice and gravy, focused on the meal. He did like this dish, though he had not made it for a while. One of the problems of having hundreds of recipes was how you sometimes forgot about some of them.

The curry was delicate, the fish's skin soft and textured. It was a tricky dish to make, because it could dry out or be overwhelmed so easily, the fish becoming nothing more than a conveyor for the curry. At which point, you lost the seafood aspect of the meal.

He'd tried adding a few other kinds of seafood to the dish—mussels and clams and even prawns—but most of them overwhelmed the balance. The clams were the best, being the least offensive, but even then, the dish as it was, with maybe a few small prawns, was the best option.

Though he had never tried adding pineapple. Again, a choice by the chef here, one that suited his clientele and his own burgeoning style. It was still raw, leaning towards perfection of taste for his clients rather than his own vision, but growing.

"Well, in a sense. It's a balance of talent and study," Henry said. "Manipulating Mana is tricky, and getting the initial start—if you're not already gifted—is the hardest. Once you have that start, then manipulating the magic in your body is easier, but it can be… uhh… hard."

Kelly frowned, then looked at Mo Meng. He kept his head down, mixing curry sauce and bok choy with his rice, ignoring the look she sent his way. He knew she wanted a further explanation, might even ask to learn it eventually. Probably.

Wished he had a better answer for her and quietly cursed the new mage.

He had forgotten they had another guest here, one of his oldest and most knowledgeable. "You're not gifted, or young enough to train." Marilyn said it simply, no rancor in her voice. "He was the same way, and what he's trying not to say was how dangerous gifting him his ability to use magic was." The old vampire shook her head. "There's a reason why mages usually come in families, because they get early training and their talent runs true. It's also the reason why science took over—it's too much work to train in volume."

"Oh..." Kelly smiled, though she was fooling no one. "I wasn't really thinking about me." Then she frowned, looking at Marilyn. "How dangerous was it?"

"With anyone but the jinn, he'd have died nine times out of ten. With the jinn..." She looked at Mo Meng for clarification and he sighed.

"Lily's always been the best of us. Probably only a one in ten chance of death or permanent injury."

Henry twitched at the words, something like dismay crossing his face. Mo Meng noted it, wondered if the jinn ever told him the dangers. Probably a little, or else he would have died already. That was the thing about gifting magic to others—it rarely went well.

Even going slowly, so many of his students had burnt themselves out. Injured or hurt themselves as they tried to do too much, too soon. Took part in wars or battles, or just tried to live their lives and were killed or driven out by the community. So many heard "magic" and believed you should be able to do everything.

And everyone forgot that even magic had limits.

It was why he preferred cooking. At least teaching people how to cook led to fewer tragedies.

An equal number of graves, though.

SEVENTEEN
Sparks

Henry finished his dish and pushed it back. The quantity was a little low, though that was, sadly, a feature of such locations. Amazing taste, low quantity. One reason why he rarely—if ever—ate at such places, even when he had the money.

Still, there was dessert left, and he had to admit he was looking forward to that.

Also he was watching Kelly now, that waitress. Curious what her reaction would be, now that she knew the cost, how much rage or disappointment there might be. To have the possibility of utilizing magic, and then have it snatched away.

"Did it hurt, then?" Kelly asked instead, surprising him.

"Hurt?"

"Having her make it possible for you to use magic?"

"I... Normally I think it does. It wasn't that bad. Just a bit of a headache..." Henry said, recalling the sharp pain, the flood of information. He touched his chest, where she had sparked it all, and felt a flicker of phantom pain, the pulse of warmth that was the Mana he now contained. A ghost of a time past, when it had hurt but... "I don't really remember anymore, in truth."

"Why?" She frowned. "Wasn't it important? Something you wanted, if you wished for it?"

"Oh, it was. Very much so. I still love it, but the pain... I guess it hurt. But you forget that, and all the other aspects. Or at least, not the degree. It hurt, but it wasn't so bad..." He struggled to explain it, struggled to describe how even on that day, so important, it had faded. Not the arguments, the laughter and the wonder and the debates on how to make it work. But... "The pain isn't important. It's in the past."

"And you weren't afraid?"

"A little, but I was mostly excited. I wasn't... I didn't really have much going for me in my life." His lips twisted wryly. "My parents were always on me, to do better. To be more."

"I know that one..." Kelly sighed. "As though finding a job that pays well is easy, or is fulfilling too." She smiled a little. "It's good to travel and see the world, if for nothing more than to experience how different people live. But it can be taken too far, too."

"Tell me about it. You get a little...rootless," Henry said, scrubbing a hand through his hair. He paused as the waiters swept in, clearing the table for those who had finished, Mo Meng the last to still be working on his plates. As he waited, Henry eyed the surroundings, his gaze drifting to the young man who sat not far away, glowering at their table, and made mental note of him. That kind was always dangerous. Unpredictable at times, and prone to a lack of control.

"Been traveling a lot?" Kelly said, curiously.

"In a way. Not far, really—mostly Europe and North America with some Asia." The look she gave him made him shrug, hunching a little. "It's mostly for work and study."

"I'm a little jealous," Kelly muttered. "So you've been studying under other people?"

Mo Meng looked up, frowned and shook his head. He finished cleaning up the last of the rice on his plate, scraping it so clean that not a single grain was left behind, before he put his utensils together, curious to hear what Henry had to say.

"When I can. It's not focused. I get a day here or there, a few weeks if I'm lucky, before I have to move on. I'm..." He frowned, ducked his head. "I'm trying to keep up."

"With Lily?" Kelly said. "Isn't she like...really good?"

"Oh, not that way!" He laughed ruefully. "I don't think I'll ever get as good as she is. I meant when she travels. She'll go to a city, and sometimes she'll spend weeks there. Other times, a day. It can be hard to keep up."

Kelly tapped her lips with one finger, a little teasing smile hidden by the motion. Certainly from Henry. "You know, girls do like being chased, but only to a certain extent."

"I don't exactly like scurrying after her either. Or cleaning up her messes. Or explaining to the locals what just happened," Henry grumped.

"Yet you do it." She cocked her head to the side now, staring at him. "Sometimes, it's better to let people make their own mistakes, you know."

"Well, I am somewhat responsible for her," Henry said.

"She's a grown woman, isn't she?"

"Yes, but—"

Speaking over him before he could continue, she added, "Then it seems like it's her responsibility to take care of her own problems. Or not."

"You don't understand. I was the one who..." He hesitated, feeling a sudden spike of interest. He turned his head to the side, noting how Marilyn and Damian were staring at him, and coughed. "I was her first friend. These days, that is."

Kelly's eyes narrowed, no longer teasing him. "It doesn't matter. At some point, even parents have to choose to let children make mistakes." A wry smile. "No matter how much they refuse or object. Or how often the children fight back. And she's no child. Even exes should be let go."

"Exes?" Henry's eyes widened and he shook his head vigorously. "No! Gods, no." He shuddered. "Wait, were you... did you?" He shuddered. "Ewww..."

"You know, I'm sure Lily will be happy to hear what you think of her," Mo Meng murmured, a glint of amusement in his eyes.

"Come on, she's my teacher. She's…Lily!" Henry said, staring at him. "You can't, you wouldn't', would you?" Now he could not help but wonder, staring at Mo Meng. He knew a little about their history. Unlike him, Mo Meng had already been an accomplished magician when he'd encountered Lily and learned from her. A little part of him wondered why he had never gifted her freedom, the way he had.

Then again, considering the nature of the chaos she was generating, perhaps that had been the wiser course. Even so…

"A gentleman does not ask."

"But does he tell?" Kelly rebutted, head propped on a hand now as she stared at her boss.

He raised a single eyebrow in reply, causing her to snort and give up. Henry was not so easily dissuaded as he added. "Please. Feel free to tell Lily I don't think of her as someone to bed." He shuddered again at the words. "But you'll have to tell me if you ever did."

"I'm not sure you understand the word *have*," Mo Meng said. "I don't have to do anything. Beyond perhaps visiting the washroom." So saying, he stood up, bowed a little. "If you'll excuse me."

Henry looked annoyed for a moment as the other man left, before he sighed and left him to it. He certainly wasn't going to chase after him, not to the washroom. Not to get an answer he didn't actually want.

Funnily enough, he noted how Damian stood up and followed. He was almost tempted, before Kelly drew his attention again. After all, she had never given a reply as to how she felt about it. And that was more interesting than anything those two might get into.

Eighteen

Growing Complications

Mo Meng waited till they were done, hands hovering over the washbasin as he tried to get the tap to trigger. Modern toys, these sensors, except half the time they did not work properly. Funny that this one was having trouble, being newly installed.

Much like the washroom itself, all black and white with a few tasteful abstract paintings. Nothing expensive, of course; and truthfully, nothing good.

He didn't feel anything looking at them, but it might just be because he wasn't the target for such things.

Too old to appreciate that kind of art.

Damian hesitated, scrubbing his hands over and over again before he spoke. "That mage with you…"

"Henry," Mo Meng said.

"Yes, Henry. Who is he?" Damian said. "He seems to know the restaurant."

"A mage of some small ability. He's connected to Lily." At the name, Damian tensed. The light in the room dimmed and shadows deepened, casting the bright lights darker and redder. Mo Meng felt a small chill roll through him, one that he kept from appearing on his face. "He works for the Mage Council on an independent basis and has visited the restaurant a couple of times. Normally with less fanfare."

"And Lily. Has she returned?" Cold fury danced in Damian's voice.

"Would it be a problem if she did?" Mo Meng tilted his head to the side. "You realize that she was—and is—an old friend. And a welcome customer."

"You let quite a few miscreants into your restaurant."

"Should I not? I am running a dining establishment, not an exclusive club."

"You do know who she is, do you not? What her presence means?" Damian grated out. "My father—the bonds that hold back many of the old ones, they all fray when magic returns."

"Yet, magic was much more available in times past." Mo Meng said. "I would say it is not more than a third as powerful as it was before. Maybe half."

"And you were happy when demi-gods, full demons and titans roamed the earth?" Damian said. "The destruction they caused—!"

"Was less than what a single bomb the mortals have built these days could do. The frequency of action in the past was certainly less than the stories you hear would make you think. Others were always watching, and if you wasted your energy on foolish displays, you were left vulnerable."

Damian looked unhappy at the answer, but he dropped the point. "What did this Henry want?"

"Henry," Mo Meng stressed the name by itself, a little portion of him amused by Damian, "is looking to learn a modification of a spell. Mage stuff. You are correct that the rising flow of energy is causing trouble. As much for the average supernatural in the hidden world as anywhere."

"How long do you think it can stay hidden, this world of ours?" Damian said. "With magic becoming more common, with various species reacquiring older gifts or their previous ones growing more powerful? How long will their willful ignorance hold?"

"I think you'd be surprised," Mo Meng said. "Nor do I think you understand how often people look aside from what might seem strange. We are a small community in a wide world."

"Really, because even your vaunted magic gave way beneath the power of their technology. They grow more dangerous each year." His lips curled up. "Have you considered what happens when they learn about us, truly? The pogroms they will launch? Once before, we hid by running into the deep wilds, but there are few enough of those anymore. Nor will we be able to hide among them, either."

"There will be pogroms. There will be countries and individuals who feel the need to act out and spew their hatred," Mo Meng agreed, softly. "We had to run before, put in place ways to help others out. But if you act on fear alone, you'll never see the good in others, either."

"And if you don't plan for the worst, when they come to take you out of the restaurant, you and Kelly will never be ready."

"Balance is always necessary," Mo Meng said. "As for my restaurant... have you not considered that places like mine are exactly the kind of places needed? To begin to allow some—if not everyone—a chance to experience a little magic, in a place of quiet and comfort? A single good memory can sometimes make a world of difference."

"I never thought you'd be so naïve."

"Naïve? Or just someone who has lived through these times before?" Mo Meng raised a hand before Damian could interrupt. "The world has changed, I agree. So much of what we knew has altered. People, though, have not. They can be great, if given the chance. They can understand others, sympathize and do the right things—if they are given the chance."

Damian shook his head, lips thinned. "Well, there's nothing I can do to change your mind. I know better than to try with you old ones."

Mo Meng smiled. "True. We are rather set in our ways. Nor do I disagree that care should be taken—I just think we should try everything else beforehand."

"And if they do come with their pitchforks and handguns?"

"Then, well, that's the reason you have two hands. One outstretched in friendship, the other with the stick." A tired exhale. "But Henry isn't the enemy, at least to us. He's trying to keep the lid on, to help those who cannot help themselves. The government might get many things wrong, but they are trying to keep a lid on things as well."

Damian shook his head, straightening. "Well, on your head be it."

Mo Meng smiled in acknowledgement. Watched as the man walked out, straight-backed, clad in designer clothing, and sighed. For all their conversation about the hidden world and the darkness approaching, he knew the man's concern had little to do with the overall future of their group; he had a more selfish and personal interest.

Mo Meng wondered if Damian himself realized that. It was quite possible the young man was fooling himself about his own interest. It was always tricky, of course, when you were of mixed parentage—the instincts of one side could easily blindside the other.

Just like his own history.

For a moment, Mo Meng stared up at the yellow fluorescent lighting. Thinking about what had been said. About the world that was changing on him, and what it meant. Then he sighed.

Perhaps it would make sense to take a few more precautions. And he knew just where to start.

After all, the kid had brought himself right to his doorstep.

Nineteen

Intermezzo

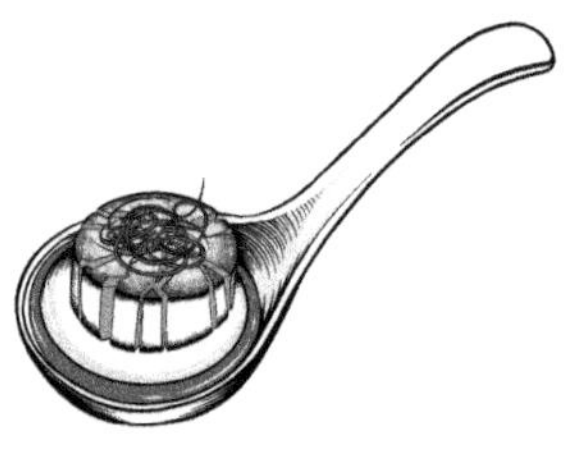

Kelly was nearly vibrating in her chair when Mo Meng finally returned. She could not help but ask, when he returned.

"What took you so long?"

"My dear, a lady never asks. Especially when the gentleman has just returned from the restroom. You never want them to hurry." Marilyn sniffed. "As it stands, few enough choose to wash properly."

"Huh?" Kelly said, surprised.

Henry was faster on the uptake; his lips twitched in humor. "She means not enough people wash their hands."

"Really?" As a food service worker, she stared at Marilyn in horror.

"Oh, yes." A slim finger rose, touched her nose. "Heightened senses can be quite useful for many things, but they can also provide some truly unwanted information."

"I... Ewww..." Kelly shuddered. "We're eating."

"That's exactly what I was thinking," Henry added.

Mo Meng stared at the group and then shook his head. "I should note that there are a number of discreet sanitation runes placed throughout my restaurant, including under tables and on chairs." He turned to Kelly. "Why are you in such a rush anyway?"

"You didn't notice?" She huffed and gestured to their surroundings. On the other tables, other diners were happily consuming the dessert that was meant for this evening. It was only their table that lacked the final course, the waiters having chosen to wait for Mo Meng's return.

Now that he had arrived, one of the men swept in, a single plate in hand. Not with the desserts, though, but with a small glass bowl with a single tiny spoon beside it, a pale scoop of fruit puree and ice lying on top. In other words, a sorbet.

"A quick intermezzo to help cleanse your palate, sir. A light lemon sorbet."

Mo Meng smiled and thanked the man, though his was the only plate delivered. He drew in a breath, noted that it lacked much smell, beyond the lightest odor of lemon rising from the dish.

No surprise; an intermezzo was meant to clear the palate. The dish was barely more than a couple of teaspoons worth of sorbet, meant to reawaken taste buds and wash down the previous dish rather than fill the stomach.

He picked up the spoon, angled it to slice off a little of the ice. It came apart with ease, the shaved ice parting with minimal effort. Popping the small spoonful into his mouth, the first thing he tasted was the lemon puree. Refreshing, slightly sour and with a trace of natural and artificial sugar, but only a hint of it. Ice melted in his mouth, filling it with little effort on his part.

Mo Meng made sure to wash the first spoonful down with a couple of sips of water, smiled a little at the annoyed huff that Kelly made as he took his time. He took a larger spoonful next, biting and chewing on the ice, enjoying the taste as the sourness of the sorbet had him salivating in moments.

"You know, this meal is taking a while. Their turn rate must be terrible," Kelly said, looking around. "Or is it just slower because it's opening night?"

"Most establishments like this expect a much slower turnover of customers," Marilyn said. "Fine dining leans towards higher prices and fewer customers overall."

"Fewer ingredients needing to be bought, then..." Kelly nodded. "And fewer dishes too, from what I can tell."

"Oh?" Henry said. "How do you know?"

"I peeked at their regular menu."

Henry looked around and Kelly shook her head. "It's online."

"Oh!" He reached towards his pocket, stopped.

Mo Meng listened idly, even as he continued to savor the dish. In moments, the sourness turned to sweet, his tongue curled up and touching the top of his mouth. He paid attention to the texture, debated if he would have gone with a thicker, coarser shaved ice for the sorbet rather than the superfine one.

It made the dish easy to consume, but lacked texture. On the other hand, it meant that within a few spoonfuls, the dish was gone. No need to wait long, though he wondered if the kitchen had to shave each one specially, since the thin ice would likely melt in moments if left sitting.

That was the problem of weighing preparation, texture and taste. You had to balance them all, and only a place like this, with a surfeit of help, could afford to weigh the decision tree in certain directions. Certainly, it was labor and time intensive in ways that his own restaurant would find impossible to meet.

Not without magic, at least. And there were limits there too, as he so often explained.

"Done?" Kelly said, waving to a waiter who was already on their way over.

Mo Meng smiled, setting the spoon down on the plate and dabbing at his mouth with the napkin. Maybe he really should look at making more desserts, if it excited her so much.

TWENTY
Dessert Arrival

K elly hovered over the plate before her, nearly bouncing in her chair as it arrived. After all, while Mo Meng made desserts, he rarely had time to produce elaborate works of art. Running a restaurant by himself limited what he could do, and often he would offer at most one or two desserts.

Sometimes he even made enough to last them a couple of days, rather than vary that portion of the menu. In his more introspective moments, he might even admit that desserts were the portion of the menu he practiced least.

Something to do with the lack of refined sugars for centuries, and the overall availability of the necessary ingredients and tools. Kelly had to admit, she'd kind of stopped listening.

Rather than a single dessert per plate, with each individual forced to make a terrible choice of which sweet they wished to test, what arrived was a single plate with three tiny desserts on it. It was the final dish of the evening, a sampler of what the full-size items might be like.

"Finally!" Kelly grinned, staring at the plate before her before she picked up the accompanying fork. Thankfully, the restaurant chose to provide constant service, sweeping in and clearing out utensils and adding in appropriate ones when necessary, rather than requiring their diners to memorize which particular utensil was to be used at what time.

Truth be told, she was not certain the vast majority of patrons knew the difference. It was one thing to be told—if you were in fact told—to eat from the outside in, but there were often a half-dozen variants of the same fork, spoons, knives ... and what about the ones that were placed diagonally at the top of the setting? It was, frankly, confusing—as it was meant to be.

One of those relics of a time when the goal was to separate the nobles and the moneyed from the hoi polloi. Except, of course, there was significantly more upward mobility in this day and age, so even the hoi polloi were able to afford to eat at these kinds of expensive dining establishments.

And capitalism, for all its faults, was more than happy to ensure that diners were comfortable and not put out by utilizing the wrong utensil, and being shamed for it. At least, not by the establishment.

"You know, attacking your dessert is not a good way of enjoying it..." Kelly said, shaking her head as she watched Henry stab his fork into the first of the desserts on his plate.

"Mmmphhfff!" At least he did not open his mouth to reply, though that might have been tricky anyway, since the chocolate delice was rich and decadent.

It amused Kelly a little to watch him gesture with his spoon in protest, even as she eyed her plate. The chocolate delice was probably the most intense of the three, with its caramel sauce and multiple layers, while the tiramisu ice cream cake was the lightest. Or perhaps that was the trifle, with its multiple layers of fruit, custard, sponge fingers and cream.

"Choices, choices, choices..." She wanted to start with the lightest, so eventually she had to go with the tiramisu ice cream cake. It was also the most likely to start melting and come apart.

She'd always been a fan of this dessert in all variations, though Kelly had to admit that the idea of an ice cream cake version of it was interesting. She scooped up the delicately arranged cake, noting the multiple distinctive layers—a dark espresso powder topping, a centimeter-thick white cream on the top, a central espresso ice cream layer, and beneath that the cake base.

Raising the forkful towards her lips, she breathed in deeply, catching the distinctive smell of espresso, rum and cream. She hesitated, breathed in again, and confirmed that she had smelled what she thought—chocolate.

Turning the fork a little, she spotted a layer at the bottom near the sponge and espresso ice cream layer. Was that a layer of chocolate to create a break, or just a natural artifact of baking the cake? Hard to tell, until she tasted it. Which, after all this hesitation, she did.

A bite, a smile.

First to come into contact, the dark espresso powder topping, instant coffee ground down to dust. Not too strong, just bitter enough to set the first taste. Then, immediately after, the white cream layer—except that was not pure cream, but ice cream. Vanilla blended into the cream to give it a little more taste, perhaps a hint of amaretto cheese, though it was hard for her to tell.

Not before the next taste, the espresso ice cream, melted and joined the others on her tongue. Unlike the bitter powder on the top, the espresso ice cream was sweet, filled with the distinctive notes of coffee and hazelnuts, before her mouth met the greater resistance of a chocolate layer, the icing splitting in her mouth with a crunch.

Then the soft sponge, soaked in dark rum and explosive with alcohol and wood flavors, moist in her mouth, the dark chocolate melting and combining with the ice cream. Each layer with a distinct flavor profile, but once it began to combine in her mouth as she chewed a little and swallowed, adding up to a new, satisfying whole.

Distinctive and familiar in taste like tiramisu, but at the same time separate because of the cold and texture and the addition of both chocolate and vanilla. Unique in a sense, but timeless. She found herself taking a third forkful in moments, barely hesitating in her movements as she enjoyed the dish.

Sugar and chocolate and coffee; she would definitely be staying up a little late tonight. Not the best option, especially when she had class tomorrow morning; but she wouldn't regret it. In fact, she started eyeing everyone else's plates.

Maybe...

A snicker from Henry brought her up short, freezing her movements, and she glared at the man. He was just a little too forward, even if he was handsome. Annoying, too, and of course; a magician. Someone who wasn't going to be around, even if he did swing by once in a while.

Still...

He did have a nice smile.

Twenty-One
A Trifling Thing

Unlike Kelly, Marilyn had not taken her time with the tiramisu. It was good, no doubt about it, but she found herself on the side of the traditionalists in this case, preferring something a little more old school. Certainly, she preferred the ladyfingers to be soaked in rum for at least a night, rather than the splash they had thrown in here.

That had been the way her family made it. Dark rum soaking into the ladyfingers at the bottom, left overnight or even a full day so that it soaked through. Barely any physical consistency left, not after being utterly drenched in rum. Heavy cream and cheese, enough sugar to rot the teeth if she had been worried about that.

One advantage of being a vampire was they actually had a significant regeneration ability. Something like teeth were a small thing to replace, and almost necessary in a sense, considering how much vampiric battles focused upon biting. The damage done to teeth by supernatural battles was considerable, and if vampires could not replace their teeth, the eldest of them would be running around like toothless hags.

While the tiramisu was tasty enough, what she was curious about was the trifle. She turned the cup around in front of her, looking at the vivid colors of the greyer tea infusion, pink rhubarb mixture, orange cream and white syllabub cream at the top. All topped off with the crunch and brown of pistachios, granola and raisins at the top.

It was a pretty dessert, possibly the best looking of the trio—after all, the chocolate delice was just chocolate, no matter what they did to brighten it up. As for the tiramisu ice cream cake, the shades of white and black were nice, but lacked a wide range of color.

In the end, though, it mattered only a little how beautiful a dessert was; what mattered more was its taste. A spoon dipped into the dessert, slicing into the depths of the cup, drawing forth a small mouthful of the dish.

She breathed in, smelled the syrup and sugar, the cream and the roasted nuts, and smiled. She opened her mouth, slipped cream and custard in and chewed on it. First came the rush of the tea, dark Earl Grey rather than jasmine or something fragrant. A heavy undertone to the dessert, broken up and intensified by the rhubarb concoction.

Her lips drew back as the sugar was amplified by the custard, soft and spongey as it broke apart in her mouth. She turned it from side to side in her mouth, cream next, and then the crunch of the roasted nuts beneath it all.

"Mmmm..." Marilyn licked her lips, smiled widely as she swallowed the mouthful. She immediately moved to take another bite, contemplating the mouthful she had just taken.

Texture, soft and creamy, sweet and roasted, the sour of the rhubarb and the infusion of tea; it was all distinctive but combined as well. Refreshing in her mouth, rather than heavy and too cold like the ice cream that came before.

A perfect summer dessert.

Another bite, and then another. She looked up, curious to see if anyone else was trying the dish. Henry was nearly done with his desserts, seeming to have chosen to eat them quickly. Mo Meng was taking his time, starting with the chocolate, and Kelly was done.

"Is it good?" Kelly said, pointing to the trifle.

"Very good. I like the use of rhubarb," Marilyn replied. "It's very Canadian."

"Not sure that was the goal," Mo Meng said. "At least, I don't believe the restaurant is trying for a local ingredient menu." A small smile on his lips. "Though, there's discussion that by eating ingredients that are naturally in season, the body is actually able to process the food."

"That..." Henry frowned, looking up. "That sounds like pseudo-science to me."

"Mmm, I have not looked into it myself. It would be interesting to see some real research eventually, when more time has passed. Much of what we believed has changed, over and over again in the last century. Two, really."

"Still, doesn't sound right." Henry paused, and added, "Or it sounds like it might be close enough to right to work."

"True. Which can be useful." When Henry gave Mo Meng a look, he chuckled. "Sympathetic magic utilizes the connection—or perceived connection—between objects to amplify their effects. A droplet of blood, a hair cutting, anything that might work. Of course, true connections are important; but if a sufficient number of people believe it, that faith can bolster the effects of the sympathy."

"So, not actually sympathetic magic alone but faith and sympathy?" Henry said, then considered his words again and winced. "That doesn't sound right."

"Yet it's true enough. What people believe to be the truth can often be as important—if not more so—as what truly is. After all, individuals act upon their beliefs, while the truth can only borrow the strength of those who will stand for it."

Henry winced. Marilyn recalled that he was working on the borders, and recalling the existing history of supernaturals and herself, she understood. Though most had lived for centuries now in relative peace with humanity, the intrinsic fear that drove others to act against the supernatural because they were the 'other' still pervaded society.

There were attempts to fix that, of course. The use of Hollywood films, of social media to offer different viewpoints, to humanize demons and vampires and more. She had been one of many who had paid for—and promoted—various vampiric TV shows and books, pushing them to the forefront. However, pervasive belief and their inability to control the overall narrative meant that there were just as many scary movies and media pushing old fears, so their work was slow.

Never mind the increasingly voluminous amount of entertainment and news options. The numerous ways individuals distracted themselves further split the narratives being told, so that Mo Meng's truth became increasingly fractured.

More, humanity was growing less and less interested in searching out truth. Life was growing ever more difficult, the pressures of existence increasing. Strangely enough, at the same time abundance was increasing at an astounding rate, but quality of life was dropping because of a confluence of factors including climate change, altering culture, demographics and greed.

Oh, so much greed.

It never ended well, of course, but humanity had the handicap of never having to live through their mistakes. Nor see the same flaws repeat, over and over again.

"But at least some things are improving…" She scraped up the last of the trifle, smiling a little. After all, what many forgot was how dire coking had been centuries ago. Few remembered how terrible simple things like sanitation in large cities were, with tens of thousands crowded together and the smell of shit and rot hanging over it all. To be replaced later by coal and wood, and then the choking miasma of lead.

No, humanity fell, and the hidden world followed. But eventually, with their help, they often managed to stagger back up. It just took time.

Twenty-Two
Chocolate Delice

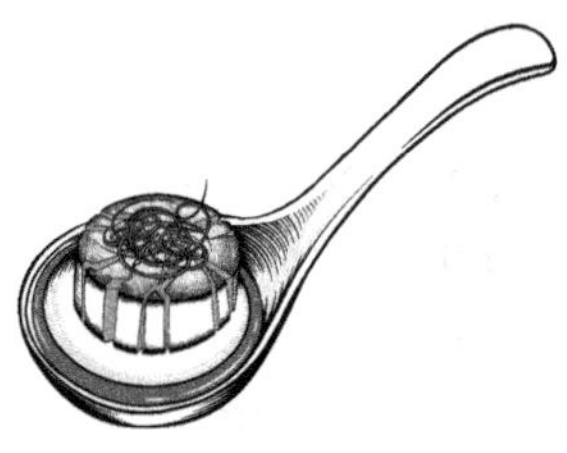

Mo Meng smiled tightly as he waved a forkful of the chocolate delice, answering Henry's question. "Exactly, the talisman will utilize a portion of sympathetic magic in its formulation. In fact, I would recommend you review the formulation itself when we begin; the last time it was checked was about two decades ago. Altering aspects of the amulet's illusion to throw off new tracking formulas would be wise."

"Definitely. I have a list of new tracking technology we'll need to cope with, from DNA to gait analysis. The question, of course, is how to alter it and what data to provide," Henry said, growing excited.

"You're thinking multi-limbed supernaturals?" Mo Meng said.

"Among others. The near-humans are close enough that spoofing to the closest mundane variation should work," Henry said. "It's those with greater variations that will be a challenge."

"True." Mo Meng finally took the bite of the delice. Derived from French patisseries, the delice was a layered dessert, this one consisting of a chocolate mousse, a layered crispy base at the bottom and a sponge right above it, and finished with a glossy ganache and oranges on the top. The restaurant had chosen to utilize both a blood and caracara orange, quickly caramelized with a blowtorch, to top it off.

It was quite an indulgent dessert and it was here that Mo Meng wondered, among the three on offer, if the restaurant had made a mistake. While each dessert was a work of art in themselves, they had certain problems.

The trifle had nuts in it, and while almond allergies were rarer, it was still a potential concern.

All three desserts were heavy cream-based, making them impossible for a vegan to consume. Or any individual with a lactose intolerance. Chocolate, while lovely and a perennial favorite, was featured in two out of three of the desserts. And only one of the desserts was gluten free—or easily made gluten free by removing the granola—and that was the trifle. The other two desserts would be problematic, unless there was a gluten free version of the tiramisu.

"Is there a gluten free version of the tiramisu? Or any of the desserts?" Mo Meng asked a waiter that he had waved over. Henry had fallen silent, muttering to himself, when he gestured the other man over. It was a good distraction since he knew the other guests in the room were fast.

"We do have gluten free versions of all the desserts," the waiter chirped. "When you supplied your RSVP, you might recall the question about allergies and food intolerances? We then catered each dish and party appropriately."

"Oh, that...makes sense," Mo Meng said, nodding. "So, dairy too?"

"We have variants that utilize plant based milk in some cases, or similar variants when necessary. In the case of the trifle, we had to make some major substitutions, but the chef believes it was more than sufficient. Would you, perhaps, care to try them, sir?"

"You're letting us have more of these desserts?" Kelly said, butting in. "Yes!"

"Ah, miss... the offer was extended to Master Mo, specifically." The waiter smiled. "But as part of his party, we would be happy to provide you variants to test yourself."

"Yes!" Kelly crowed.

Mo Meng nodded as well, amused but happy to agree to this. Not that he particularly needed to eat more—he generally did not consume that much—but it would be rude not to test out these allergy free versions. He himself had not spent much time learning or balancing out such recipes, especially for desserts, but knew they were a challenge.

That was not to say he disliked the delice, either. It was quite a bold dessert, the chocolate mousse thick and creamy and breaking apart only with some effort. The hardened layer of chocolate and softer sponge at the bottom were less intense than the chocolate mousse, a hint of coffee in the dish giving it a subtle layering of flavor. Vanilla, of course, inside the mocha sponge cake, which was not surprising. And while the main chocolate mousse was a milk chocolate, the ganache on top was pure dark chocolate; probably in the 80% cocoa range. Not bitter, however, just intense.

If it was all just chocolate, even different layers of it, the dish would have been rather one-note—even with the addition of the mocha and vanilla. However, the addition of a small amount of strawberry puree and sauce on the outside, drizzled on the side of the plate, allowed Mo Meng to test a different, sharper flavor on top of it.

And then, of course, there were the oranges. Blood and caracara, two different types of oranges. Blood oranges an interesting variant, not as sweet and the bright colors often off-putting for some diners, but set against the darkness of the chocolate, it was bright and inviting.

Placed on a heated surface for a few seconds, just enough to caramelize the outside, the oranges had that touch of burnt texture and taste that came from the melted sugars, the sharp acidity and the sweetness that arose from it, all combining with the chocolate variations and the occasional swipe of the delice across the strawberry puree to break up the monotony of the chocolate.

"So I take it the delice meets your standards?" Marilyn teased as he finished swiping up the last of the strawberry, popping the remainder of the dish into his mouth.

Mo Meng chewed, swallowed, drank a sip of water and smiled. "It's good. The use of the oranges—caramelized as they are—is very smart. A little heavy for a finale for dinner, and maybe a touch sweet for my personal taste, but I can see this being a popular dish with diners."

"So, good but not good enough for you." Marilyn propped her head on one hand, as she picked at her own dish. Beside them, even Kelly's greed had hit her limit and now she was negotiating with Henry about what and how much he could eat to help her finish the dish. Why she didn't just leave it uneaten, Mo Meng was uncertain, though he was not about to complain about her scruples. "What would you do, if you were going to make this?"

Mo Meng shook his head. When she continued to stare at him, he explained out loud. "No idea. I'd have to test a few variants. I think making the base even more different would be good. Maybe adding another layer, something cream or berry based to help alter the texture. It's hard to say, and it would depend on the end goal." He shrugged. "It's a matter of taste, too. I don't like it when it's too sweet."

"Typical Chinese."

"Exactly," Mo Meng answered. "So something less sweet, maybe add a bit more texture. I do like the use of oranges, but I wonder about the puree. Then again, people pay to eat triple chocolate delights."

Marilyn's eyes narrowed and she laughed, shaking her head in amusement. It was, she had to admit, typical of the man.

TWENTY-THREE
A Fine Night Out

Kelly groaned, holding her stomach as she stepped out into the cold spring evening from the double glass doors that separated Rõõmu from its surroundings. Night had fallen in the time they had been inside, though the air conditioning had kept the inside to a reasonable temperature. Out here, though, she shivered and wished she had brought along a shawl – or, better yet, a coat.

"You okay?" Henry said, stepping close to her.

"I'm fine. Just a little cold." She smiled at the man, then blinked as Damian, detaching himself from where he had been standing waiting for his car to arrive, coughed.

"Here." Damian began to unsling his jacket, and Kelly shook her head.

"I'm okay," she refused automatically.

"I've got it." Henry smiled at the other man, nodding back in the direction that Damian came from. "You might want to give it to her, though."

Damian's date was glaring at his back, the woman in a red dress made with about half the amount of fabric as Kelly's. She had thought she was being daring, wearing something so tight, but Damian's date had obviously been out to impress.

Kelly had to admit, she had done well. Maybe a little too much makeup, though she had an impression Damian liked them a little more made-up. But she was obviously a devotee of the gym and had the body—and heels—to prove it.

The moment Damian turned back, she was all smiles, grateful to take the coat. But Henry was shaking his head judgmentally.

"That's not going to last."

"Not sure it's meant to," Kelly said, quietly. "Now, if you would..." She shivered again, rubbing her arms.

"Oh, right." A hand rose, waved, and she felt something wrap itself around her, warming her immediately.

"What is that?" A warm coat that moved with her as she waved her hand around a little.

"Simple spell for warmth," Henry said. "It'll last for about an hour before it goes away." He hesitated, then added, "If you need it gone before then, just flick your fingers three times." He demonstrated, putting middle finger to thumb and flicking it three times in rapid succession.

"Oh, that's convenient." Kelly raised her hand, almost tempted to try it herself, but wisely choosing not to.

"Good practice, too." Mo Meng smiled, exiting at last. He had been caught by the chef as dinner ended, dragged into the kitchen and introduced around. Marilyn had slipped away, muttering something about seeing them soon, but Kelly had chosen to linger behind.

"Oh?" she asked, hoping for clarification.

"Personal magic layered on someone else should always have an end point and a way for the recipient to turn it off. Unless you're intending to lay a curse, of course." At the look the pair gave him, he shrugged. "Surely you've heard of dancing shoes that force the wearer to continue dancing forever. Or cookpots that constantly boil over." Eyes narrowing in humor, he added. "I'm sure Disney made a cartoon about it." A lip twitched. "If I was still teaching, I would probably make watching it one of my first lessons."

"Mickey Mouse?" Henry said, amused. "We're taking lessons in magic from Disney?"

"Words of wisdom, if nothing else." Mo Meng shrugged. "You'd be surprised how much of magic is common sense. And how often not using magic is the right thing to do."

"So you've mentioned." Henry sighed. "So has Lily."

"Get old enough, you learn most of the same lessons." He sighed. "If you're willing to listen." Mo Meng frowned. "And are willing to change."

"So, maybe not, then?" Henry grinned, teasing.

"Fine. People are people, and even old ones might have different views of the world." Mo Meng sighed. "Though some things hold true, if you do survive." A hand raised, waved. "Don't worry about it. Now, you had a question for me?"

Henry nodded, then paused and looked at Kelly hesitantly.

She smiled brightly at the pair. "Now that I'm warm, and too full, I'm going to walk home."

"You know, it's a little late..." Henry hesitantly began.

"Oh? You think I don't know how to walk home in my own city?" She snorted. "You know I work in a restaurant, right? I go home late at night six days a week. Sometimes seven."

"Six?" He turned to look at Mo Meng, frowning. "You have her working six days a week?"

"I don't have her doing anything," Mo Meng replied. "She sets her own schedule."

"And the one day I was ill last month, my phone blew up with complaints."

"Which I told you, you should shut off."

"Uh huh." Kelly crossed her arms. After a moment, she laughed. "Whatever. Maybe we can talk about work-life balance once Damian is up to speed." She smiled a little fondly in the direction the man had disappeared in, having driven off in a car that she was certain cost more than the apartment she rented. "Nor am I disliking the overtime and tips."

"Right..." Henry answered. Toronto was an expensive city to live in, after all.

"Now shoo, you two go talk magic."

Waving a hand, she strolled away, leaving the pair of bemused mages. She stretched a little, her small clutch swinging as she strolled. The magic was rather nice, if she said so herself. Warming like a hug. Even better, she would get home long before midnight. Which meant she'd have a chance to catch up on her TV.

Or mindlessly doomscroll. Either, or.

Whistling a tune to herself, she patted her too-full stomach as she walked home, eyeing the clear sky. There definitely were some nice perks to this job. While eating was fun, she found herself looking forward to getting back to work soon and serving some amazing dishes.

For all the fanciness of Rõõmu, she rather preferred the more down-home aspect of the Nameless Restaurant. Anyway, she had a feeling from the gleam in Mo Meng's eye as he exited that he was cooking up some new dishes.

Change was coming to the restaurant and the world. The only question was how much and in what direction.

###

The End

Look out for the next exciting installment in
Magical Mains

www.starlitpublishing.com/products/magical_mains

Want to read a bonus scene featuring Henry & Mo Meng?

Join my newsletter to get the exclusive content. www.mylifemytao.com/bonus-epilogues

Let's stay connected
Be the first to hear about new books, special offers, and behind-the-scenes extras.

Author's Note

Thank you for reading Sorcerous Plates.

It was a little bit of a change of pace when writing this, compared to the other Hidden Dishes novellas, in that Mo Meng is not cooking the meals. Strangely enough, I had started writing a different work but was finding it quite hard going, what with the similar settings.

Changing it up, making Mo Meng the diner and being inspired by a lovely meal with my wife actually gave me the impetus to write the work you hold in your hands. It's a little less hands-on, since the level of cooking required to reach Michelin Star works is alien to me. I'm more of a home cook, so while I can base it off what I've seen, what I've read and what I've experienced, I could only extrapolate so much.

Hopefully, it was enjoyable anyway.

The series has a few more works before I'm done. I always had a specific ending for the series, and I think I need at least one more 'set-up' novella before I can write the final one. I'm leaning towards two, making for a total of 7 works in the Hidden Dishes series and a complete arc.

If you enjoyed everything you've read, do join my newsletter. I've got a lot of other works coming out, both in bookstores and online, and many more exciting works to tell you about.

Hopefully, you'll continue to follow along the adventures of Mo Meng and the staff of the Nameless Restaurant.

And again, thank you, for all your support.

~Tao

About the Author

Tao Wong is the author of the *A Thousand Li* progression fantasy series and the *System Apocalypse* LitRPG series, among others. His work has been released in audio, paperback, hardcover, and ebook formats, and translated into German, Spanish, Portuguese, Russian, and several other languages. He was shortlisted for the UK Kindle Storyteller Award in 2021 for *A Thousand Li: The Second Sect*. In 2026, the first three books in the *A Thousand Li* series will be republished in hardcover by Ace Books.

When he's not writing or working, he enjoys practicing martial arts, reading, and dreaming up new worlds. He lives in Toronto, Canada.

Please check out *A Gamer's Wish* – book 1 of the Hidden Wishes Series.
https://books2read.com/u/3LKZMX

For updates on the series and his other books (and special one-shot stories), please visit the author's website: http://www.mylifemytao.com

Subscribe to Tao's mailing list to receive exclusive access to short stories in the Thousand Li and System Apocalypse universes.

If you'd like to support Tao directly, he has a Patreon page - benefits include previews of all his new books, full access to series short stories, and other exclusive perks. Tao Wong Patreon

Or visit Tao's Facebook Page:
www.facebook.com/taowongauthor/

For more great information about LitRPG series, check out these Facebook groups:

- GameLit Society

  www.facebook.com/groups/LitRPGsociety

- LitRPG Books

  www.facebook.com/groups/LitRPG.books

About the Publisher

Starlit Publishing is wholly owned and operated by Tao Wong. It is a science fiction and fantasy publisher focused on the LitRPG & cultivation genres. Their focus is on promoting new, upcoming authors in the genre whose writing challenges the existing stereotypes while giving a rip-roaring good read.

For more information on Starlit Publishing, visit our website! www.starlitpublishing.com

You can also join Starlit Publishing's mailing list to learn of new, exciting authors and book releases.